DEPARTURE LOUNGE

Chad Taylor

DEPARTURE LOUNGE

Europa
editions

Europa Editions
116 East 16th Street
12th floor
New York, N.Y. 10003
www.europaeditions.com
info@europaeditions.com

The author gratefully acknowledges
the assistance of Creative New Zealand.

Library of Congress Cataloging in Publication Data is available
ISBN 1-933372-09-5

Taylor, Chad
Departure Lounge

Book design by Emanuele Ragnisco
www.mekkanografici.com

Printed in Italy
Arti Grafiche La Moderna – Rome

For Debra

DEPARTURE LOUNGE

Prologue: 1979

The TV news reader is wearing a suit and tie. At the end of the bulletin he looks down from the auto cue to read from a sheet of paper. He says Flight 901 to the Antarctic scheduled to land in Christchurch at 7 p.m. is three hours late. He pauses then as if he is about to add something, but doesn't. He puts the sheet of paper down and turns to the weather girl and says: and now for today's weather.

The weather girl clasps her hands in front of her midi skirt as she reads out the summer temperatures. The painted map behind her is draped with spiked magnetic lines. She looks strained as she moves southward through the regions.

When she comes to Gisborne and stretches out her left hand, her fingers are trembling. Towards the bottom of the North Island her voice is trembling as well. She blinks as she speaks to the camera. By the time she comes to summarise the temperatures in the four main centers her voice is breaking. The weather girl is crying.

The TV camera cuts back to the newsreader. He repeats that the flight to Mount Erebus, Antarctica is late with 237 listed passengers and twenty crew on board. The news reader says good night.

1.

The Ponsonby Nine Billiards Lounge was not a rough place. There was a plastic eight ball hanging over the street door and a neon cactus quivering in the window beside it. The "Nine" in the name came after the number of tables inside: eight with green baize spaced symmetrically along either side of the attic room and one blue at the end. A sign at the top of the stairs said *No Betting, Friendly Games Only*. The bar sold American beer and the jukebox was stacked with country music nobody really liked.

Despite that, a nice little crowd had gathered there to play pool in the hours between midnight and dawn. The space was filled with the soft crackle of balls being knocked across the felt. The narrow tin lampshades draped shadows across the different players, separating their faces from their playing arms and scattering them in the darkness.

Two businessmen had turned up to stretch their working day a little longer, pegging their suit jackets on the rack where the bowed cues were slotted into brackets. The man with a wedding band had tucked the end of his tie into his breast pocket. The one with shorter hair had rolled up the sleeves of his shirt to show off the little skull tattoo on his arm. His pale face flinched as he drew back for the break.

The fat player on table three had a tan and the greasy black scratches on his hands that you get from working on a boat. His skinny opponent was wearing a Hawaiian shirt despite the cold outside. The bones of his left wrist stuck out where it had snapped once and healed up the wrong way. The fat guy liked to line up his shots cack-handed and roll them slowly across the green while the Hawaiian preferred to slam them down. They were taking their time in the manner of old friends. While one took his turn the other would glare at the table as if mapping its shiny patches and dots. The Hawaiian was ahead. The expression on their faces said both of them were losing.

Three women were sharing the same game on table five. Even from a distance it was obvious that the youngest of them had never played before. She had a technique of either missing the white or hitting it so hard it that jumped off the table and bounced along the floor. Her friends were taking it in turns to coach her but their advice wasn't doing much good. One was smoothing things over by squealing when her friend missed and the other was jangling her bracelets. They were having a good time. The bracelet-rattling alone was sending the skull tattoo businessman's game to hell.

Rory Jones and I were playing on the blue table. Rory had also hung his Italian jacket on the cue rack and was standing there with one finger hooked in his belt. His cuffed pants had been tailored to break perfectly across his shiny little French shoes. Rory's hair was thick and wavy, like a child's. Every few minutes he would take his fingers out of his pants and rake them through his hair as if he was checking that it was still there. I stood and listened, squinting with interest as Rory told the story of the first day he became involved in property.

* * *

Rory got his start when the old George Courts store on K Road closed its doors. He had no money. He paid the deposit with his credit card and went looking for investors. Three weeks later he was selling his Mercedes to cover the interest when a buyer called to offer twice what he'd paid. Twice. Rory closed the deal and walked out of the dealership with a brand new coupé. The experience confirmed what he had always believed: there were no rewards for being cautious.

Rory's next deal was the Delta apartments on Viaduct Quay. After Delta, there was V-City behind Victoria Park and the Onslow Village on Richmond Road. The projects were apartment buildings with courtyards and narrow car parks and tiny balconies. Rory called them lifestyle projects: all the style of city living without the responsibility.

Although Onslow Village looked old-fashioned, it went up overnight. Rory built the project on soggy land on the slope in Richmond Road. He reclaimed with fill from the Auckland casino. He trucked the casino dirt across town and piled it onto the bog where it formed a smooth, brown mound. The mound became spiked with grass in spring. In summer the rains came and tamped it down again, and then Rory started building.

Onslow was built with the latest techniques. For the foundations, Rory explained, they pegged out the dirt with string, then laid polystyrene cubes in lines and then poured cement all around and over the cubes. It was like using ice cubes to build a freezer tray.

"You can do the foundations in days," Rory said. "You bury the plumbing and wires in the cement, staple the walls and ceiling on top and start wheeling in the tenants." He snapped his fingers. "And that's it."

The Onslow apartments were Tuscan style, which meant they had thick walls that looked like stone or adobe. In reality the walls were wooden box frames covered with plywood and plaster. The timber used to build the frames was untreated, to save money, and assembled with hydraulic nail guns and cleats in order to save time. The places looked fashionable and sold for a lot of money. Rory's clients were mostly either elderly couples retiring to the inner city or newlyweds investing in a first home.

His buyers, however, never got the chance to sell. Eighteen months after Onslow was finished the first balconies began to collapse. The cheap cladding admitted rain. The moisture rotted the untreated timber. The rot was incubated by the humid Auckland weather, and the mould became toxic. Beneath the salmon-coloured cladding Onslow was rotting away like a bad tooth. Less than a year after moving in the tenants were staring at repair bills worth more than their mortgage. Some of them had taken legal action and formed a collective to sue. Rory was unconcerned.

"I set up a limited company to develop the investment," he said. "Onslow Developments. I didn't build Onslow Village: Onslow Developments did. Onslow Developments got sign off from the city planners and inspectors. Onslow Developments paid the builders and landscape gardeners, and Onslow Developments sold the properties. Not me, not my lawyer, not any of my investors. Ons-low." He poked the blue surface as he pronounced each syllable. "Those people bought from Onslow. Their problem's with Onslow."

Rory scooped up the balls and dropped them into the wooden triangle, rolling their chipped numbers and stripes into position.

"So where's Onslow now?" I said.

"The company returned its investment and was liquidated. It doesn't exist."

"So you don't owe anyone," I said.

"Not a cent." He lifted the triangle away and stood back from the table. "Your break."

I took it.

"That's what the entity was for, you see," he said, watching the five ping back and forth inside the pocket without going in. "Onslow as a company existed to build the apartments under the regulations and nothing more. The full extent of its liability has been discharged under law."

"But the owners are still angry."

He spread his hands. "Mark: we're all disappointed. But these building techniques were the best of their day. The city council engineers signed them off—qualified people. We trusted them. I trusted them. Shit, I don't know anything about building. Look at me. Do I look like a fucking labourer?"

"No," I said. "You don't."

"No offence."

"None taken."

He stuck out his bottom lip. "If I found a bad patch on the floor, sure, I'd be angry. I'd want someone to fix it. But the legal reality is that it's not really someone else's problem, and they know that, and that's why they're upset: they know they have to make the repairs."

"Right."

"You can see it, right? If they knew, deep down, that it wasn't their problem, why would they be angry?"

"Right."

"We live in the real world," he said. "We're all grown-ups here. Nobody's holding our hand. But I tell you something: every one of those people has insurance. Every one of them still has an asset. Maybe it's depreciated but the market fixes everything in the long term. Was it a good investment? Yes. Was it a gamble? Definitely. Everything's a gamble. There is no gain without risk. There's no life without risk. It's like my first investment: that was a huge risk. Huge. I didn't sleep. I thought I was going to die. But I went for it and I won, and that's why I'm living like I live now. You know where I was before I came tonight?"

"No."

"I was at Cruz. You know it?"

Cruz was a three star that had just opened down on the Viaduct: not the freight docks or the marina where the trailer sailors went but the new part where the big yachts lay waiting for their owners to be helicoptered in. Cruz had oval windows and a balcony that stuck out over the water. The waitresses were pale and hungry looking. The diners had tans in winter and bread with everything.

"Don't know it," I said. "Is it nice?"

"It's okay." Rory shrugged. "I was there with these two guys I do business with, with their girlfriends, you know—a business dinner. Very pleasant. Beautiful wine, beautiful food, great atmosphere. Beautiful. And we're talking business and then halfway through the meal we concluded it and you know what I did? I walked out. I said thanks, I'm finished doing business, it was a beautiful meal, great to meet you and now I have to go. And I got in my car and I drove up to Ponsonby to shoot some pool with some real people, you know? To experience some real atmosphere, have a real conversation with someone like yourself—not some bullshit thing about this wine or this entrée or blah, blah. The dots on your knuckles: they're jail tattoos. Right?"

"Right."

"Please: don't be embarrassed. I'm very observant. Property is people: people are property. To do what I do, I've gotta know both."

He eyed up the five sitting on the edge of the pocket and gave it just enough of a nudge for it to bounce out again. He stood up and shook his head.

"You think I'm going on about it," he said.

"It's an emotional issue."

"Hey, Mark—you know what? You're exactly right." He tapped the lampshade. "That's the very point I make to people every day. Property is emotion. It's who we are. It's how we feel. It's our identity. Not just the land and the people: the very house. You move into a big house, you become a louder person. Maybe you move into a new place, you attract new people and gradually, over time, you change: you become new. So what are we saying is effecting this change: the person, or the space around them? It's not a lounge: it's us. That's why I got into this line of work, Mark. Property is our modern religion."

He looked back again at the blonde girl sitting at the bar.

"Is it her shot or yours?" Rory said.

Josie Richmond smiled back at us, bored. Her hair had been chemically straightened and her business suit had been dry-cleaned and her face was the shape of a new apple. The crease in her smile came from her father's side of the family. Her family made wine in Hawke's Bay. She had a passport photo of herself in her pocketbook aged nine, gap-toothed in the dappled light of the vines. She could cash it in and go back home anytime.

"She's not playing," I said.

I walked around and picked the 11. It bobbed off the cushion. Rory glanced back at Josie, then at me.

"So what's the story there?" he said.

I didn't bite.

"You didn't sink anything, right?" Rory said.

"No."

He bent over and popped in the ten.

"You're unders," he said.

I let Rory win the next frame. He wasn't a bad player. His hands shook when he got cocky, which put him at a disadvantage when he was winning. The way to beat him would have been to let him get way ahead and wait until he fell apart— assuming I was good enough to come back at him. I'd sort of lost track over the course of the evening in favour of concentrating on every dumb thing that Rory was saying. He kept raking his fingers through his hair and stealing glances at Josie and Josie carried on sipping her beer, just enough to whet her whistle but not enough to get drunk. The three of us kept on at it for a good hour before we quit. Afterwards Rory and I agreed to meet up again, both of us knowing we wouldn't. And then the following night, I broke into his apartment and stole everything that wasn't nailed down.

2.

Rory's building was a sleek grey box five storeys high. It stood across from the motorway off-ramp on the fashionable, slightly rough part of town.

I approached it from the motorway side. Over winter the parkies and street kids had built a second city under the bridge but had abandoned it in late October. The flattened boxes and plastic bag curtains were empty. Either the nights had become more forgiving or the police had moved them on. The bridge supports were still black with graffiti. Cigarette stubs and beer cans were scattered around. I sat down beside a scorched ring of dirt and looked across to where Rory lived.

The main entrance to the building was on the ground floor. The courtyard was ringed by a stone wall. The garage was sealed by a roller cage. The windows were double-glazed to cut out the noise. A second wire fence at the bottom of the hill stopped the litter blowing across and dirtying the tenants' view.

Rory was right when he said houses are like people. Every place has its own personality. Some attract attention and others don't. Some never get touched and others get done over and over, like the kid everyone bullies at school. The pattern has nothing to do with the locks or the alarms. There's no logical reason for it. You just get a feeling that a place is right.

Once you've made your pick, it's good to spend some time learning everything you can. It doesn't take long to work out what's going on inside. You take a position somewhere near the property and spend a few hours watching who comes in and out, how many keys they use on the door, whether or not they close the bathroom window—that sort of thing. Old properties especially have all sorts of quirks: back doors that have been nailed shut; sash windows that jam. They clench like an old grey fist that doesn't want to let go.

Rory left around midnight. The garage door rolled up and Rory drove out, the engine of his latest Mercedes humming a mild tune. He turned up the hill and sped away. I thought he was maybe a little short on the clutch.

He had left plenty of empty spaces behind inside the garage. I did a quick count before the roller door lowered again. Rory preferred neighbours who had the money to take holidays and dine out on weeknights. Which was good, I thought. Living in the city, you need to get out. The numbers in the slots corresponded to the numbers of the apartments, which was also good.

I stood up and stamped the dust to get the cramp out of my legs. Then I climbed down the hill. Behind me the traffic roared like the air sweeping off a wing.

* * *

The lobby doors were strengthened glass. I counted the mailbox slots that were jammed with junk mail. I put my hand over the lens on the intercom and started pressing buttons, scratching the microphone if someone answered. The third person to respond figured it for a malfunction and buzzed me straight in. And that was it. One person is all it takes. The stone and steel gave the place atmosphere, though.

I ignored the lift. The fire escape stairs ran the height of the building, with plenty of places to hide. I trotted up to Rory's door and knocked. There was no reply.

The lock was a solid push-button combination. I scraped some billiard chalk into my palm. The blue dust stuck to the grease of the four buttons Rory pressed every time he opened the door. It didn't take much to unscramble them: the date of Rory's first real estate deal. I punched it in. The door opened.

Rory's penthouse was a single apartment but he had squeezed a whole mansion in there. A walnut-lined foyer led into the lounge and dining area. A spiral staircase curled up towards a bedroom on the mezzanine. The lights were recessed. The spaces between the ceiling beams had been cut out and installed with skylights. The brick walls had been scraped back with a melon spoon.

I found a pair of washing gloves from the kitchenette and pulled them on. There was a good Ginsu knife in the drawer as well. I stuck that in my back pocket.

The stereo speakers were hidden in the walls. The player and tuner were out in the open. I wrenched the components free and stacked them by the door. I picked the giant white vase up off the sideboard and raised it above my head and dropped it on the wooden floor. Inside was a bag of dope, some pills and Polaroids of Rory's girlfriends. He had focussed mainly on their chest and waist areas but there were three girls, from what I could see, reclining on the same red background. I arranged them on the couch in a nice heart shape before going upstairs.

The double bed had a red cover that matched the background in the photos. The attic windows opened out onto a mock balcony with a view of the breezeway. From the closet I took the Polaroid camera, a Nikon, a watch collection (Hermès, Rolex, Bulgari) in a lined wooden box, Rory's business cards and a frankly reckless amount of cash.

I dwelled for a moment over his passport. Rory was a reasonably well-known man but the people who'd be buying a passport probably wouldn't know that. I stuffed it in my back pocket. The handcuffs, I left. Everything else I wrapped in a bedsheet and carried downstairs.

It had taken me less than twenty minutes to roll Rory's apartment. My heart was pounding. I stood in the downstairs car park staring at the empty spaces, counting the numbers and wondering who they stood for. Half the building was empty. It was a good time of night. It was worth going back for another bite.

* * *

I knocked on the first door just to be sure. The lock was standard and the frame was light. I jammed the Ginsu into the moulding and wedged it wide enough to trick the bolt.

Inside was dark. The place smelled like patchouli. I shut the door behind me and tilted the blinds to let in the night. The furniture was a smoked glass table and brown leather chairs. I grabbed the DVD. I tossed the bedroom dresser. I kicked the shoes out of the wardrobe to make sure there was no floor safe. I found two good watches and a lot of silver and three Indonesian passports: two adults and a child. I zipped the passports into my jacket pocket. I carried the rest downstairs in a pillow case and sat in the parking spot to catch my breath.

Too good.

I went back up.

The third place smelled of air freshener and cigarettes. It had pot plants and rattan furniture and the walls were covered with photographs. There were dozens of them, all in black and white: white mountains; a grey marketplace; a white girl in a black kimono. The TV was a new wide-screen and too heavy to carry. The VCR was old. Whoever lived here had put all their money into the photos. Maybe they were worth something, but not to me. I found a laptop and a cell phone that I wrapped in a leather suit bag. The passport had expired. I pocketed the credit cards.

It was still quiet in the car park. I dumped the suit bag next to the other bundles and shook the sweat out of the rubber gloves. Spots fell on the cement floor. My hands were hot but everything else felt cool. I was on a roll, now. This was Sunday shopping. I was hitting my stride.

I checked out the back, through the fire escape door. Traffic was rushing along the bridge. The rest of the street was still dark. I had a good haul and every reason to leave it at that. But I didn't. I took a deep breath and went back inside.

* * *

I went upstairs to one last door and knocked. There was no reply. I put my ear to it. It sounded quiet enough. I jammed the lock and stepped in and shut the door silently behind me.

The place smelled like old flowers. I tilted the blinds and orange light washed across the room.

The funeral director had left his business card in an ashtray on the kitchen bench. Next to the ashtray was a pair of folded reading glasses, the lenses staring at the ceiling.

The apartment was filled with boxes. The cartons by the door were taped shut and labelled: *Dishes. Books. Clothing.* The old-fashioned furniture had been pushed into the center of the lounge. The seat cushions had been removed from the chairs and stacked in front of the balcony window. A set of shelves had been unscrewed from the walls. Ornaments lay around waiting to be wrapped in tissue and newspaper.

A note taped on the unplugged television set said *Sold.* The stereo was labelled *Salvation Army.* The kitchen drawers were empty. The books were stacked in the middle of the floor. The funeral director had hired the movers to box everything up and take it away. By tomorrow the last possessions would be gone.

Up on the motorway the cars were slipping by, their head-lights travelling across the wall but there was a stillness in the room, now. Since I entered, something had changed.

The bedroom had been dusty for a long time. The old man wouldn't have noticed. The mattress had been stripped. The dresser mirror had corroded so that little bits of the reflection had fallen away. There was borer in the wood. The empty drawers were lined with fine grey powder. His wife's jewellery was paste and jet.

The second bedroom had yet to be cleared. The smell was stronger in there: old blankets and clothing and watery perfume. I ran my fingers between the slats of the blinds. The motorway lights rippled across the bed.

There were dolls on the shelves and ornaments on the dresser. Children's artwork was pinned on the walls: crayon outlines of a hand on crinkled sheets of newsprint; dabs of bright paint. There were paintings of flowers and trees and Auckland harbour. There was a picture of Rangitoto Island, the volcano's peak sticking out of the soft, friendly sea. They were signed by a name: Caroline.

Caroline May.

The teenager's clothes in the closet smelled of mothballs. A Keep On Truckin' T-shirt, bellbottomed jeans. At the back of the closet were more boxes filled with clothes and photographs.

I shook some of the photos out. Caroline's primary school portraits were in little white and gold frames. As I flicked through them, she grew older through the years. First she had round cheeks, then no front teeth, then her teeth grew back, then her hair grew long. It got long enough so she held it back with a band, and then plaits. She got taller. She went to intermediate school, then high school.

The class photo had faded since 1979. Caroline was smiling in the back row, right next to me. I was smiling too. I dusted both our faces clear. There was a lot of dust. It was a long time ago.

3.

North Head stood at the mouth of Waitemata Harbour, a natural fortification. After the Europeans settled in Auckland in the nineteenth century the navy dug gun emplacements into the peak to prepare for a Russian invasion. In World War II the guns were replaced with more powerful versions to repel the Germans and the Japanese. The attacks never came.

As a result the head was criss-crossed with tunnels and underground passages that linked the years of fortification. Its grassy slope eroded in steps, staggering around the cement bunkers. The sea wall collected graffiti and barnacles and green slime from the salt spray. The oysters along the rocks turned brown with runoff. The T-shaped gun slots were streaked with verdigris that looked like sad faces, empty and staring at the gulf.

The cracked streets that ran through the suburb surrounding North Head was a reminder of the region's age. The poured black sidewalks had been baked by years of summers. The trees were bent wire that turned red in the sunset.

The village used to be a centre for boat-building until the industry shifted from wooden hulls to metal and the business slid over to the city side of the harbour. Now trademark industry was reduced to a luxury or a quirk: the pursuit of people with either too much money or no proper job. But anything stronger than a breeze still rocked the dozens of small craft moored in the bay, wagging their masts like tails. The crazy and wealthy alike gathered on the banks above the sand spit to paint and scrape and saw, but they spent more time repairing their boats than they did sailing them.

The closest most residents got to the water was the workers' ferry that connected the city and the shore. The old green and white boats with their trails of rust departed on the hour from the city terminal. The journey across the harbour took 25 minutes in a bad chop. The wharf was an old tin shed that ran the length of the jetty. Birds nests plugged the holes in the roof. The old wooden seats were as worn as a church pew.

On the street where Caroline May lived the settler villas were painted in hippy colours: purple weatherboards, green sashes, bright red doors. The branches of the lemon trees were grey. The rock walls were spotted in lichen and the clipped front lawns grew thick. Wildflowers sprouted along the edges of the steps, sprinkling them with yellow.

Caroline used to walk the dog with her parents when she was young but they were left with the chore now that she was older. She was lying on the sofa in the lounge listening to her brother's copy of *Pet Sounds* and chewing a strand of her long blonde hair. Mrs. May leaned through the door to say they were going out. She asked her daughter to put on something warmer: her thin cotton blouse and elephant bells were far too thin. Mrs. May said it was winter but Caroline said it was nearly spring. Mrs. May asked her to turn the music down but Caroline said it wasn't loud. Mrs. May kept on and on about it like she always did until Caroline ended the argument by rolling over on the couch and turning her back to the door.

The Council signs along the track leading to the beach said it was illegal for dogs to go without a leash but the Mays let the lab run loose the same as everyone else in the neighbourhood. The dog knew his way: they didn't have to watch where he went. They walked with their heads down and their hands in their pockets, shrugging off the wind.

Rain had darkened the sand above the tide line. A man in a hooded oilskin was walking at the other end of the beach, and there was a woman with her two children in brightly coloured windbreakers. There may have been other couples on the beach, but they couldn't have said for certain. A Sunday walk was a Sunday walk. They enjoyed the stroll regardless.

They paid no attention to how long they walked or how far. They didn't notice what caused them at some stage to decide to turn back. When asked later, they would never be able to recall who else was on the beach at that point.

The dog reached the house first. It shook itself clean on the lawn. Mr. and Mrs. May walked around the back of the house and knocked the sand off their shoes. The fine mesh insect screen that hung across the back door was unlatched and the door itself was unlocked. The lights were off downstairs but it hadn't started to get dark. Mrs. May called out to her daughter that they were back. There was no reply, but there was nothing unusual about that. Lately, Caroline had started to ignore most people.

Mr. May spooned out the dog's food on the back step. The dog wagged its tail and bumped its master's legs, trying to reach the soft roll.

Mrs. May started making dinner. She heated the oven and pasted fat in the baking tray and then picked up the joint she had left out to thaw on the kitchen bench. The meat was soft and blood had pooled dark red on the orange and yellow patterned plate. She cut away the plastic wrapping with a short knife and held the limb up to let the blood run off before she laid it in the tray. She threw salt on the meat and covered it with a cloth until the oven had come to heat. The dog could smell the blood. She put the plate on the floor and let the dog lick it clean.

When Mrs. May next noticed the clock on the stove it read 4:30 p.m. She looked around to see if her daughter had slipped by to avoid making conversation, as had been her tendency in recent months, but she hadn't. Mrs. May wiped her hands and went into the lounge and asked her husband if Caroline had come through. Mr. May looked up from the TV and said no. Mrs. May watched the people sliding left and right across the screen. She ran the cotton cloth between her fingers, around her wedding ring. She went back into the kitchen and started peeling potatoes. The whine of the cars faded in and out on the other side of the door. The meat was cooking.

When it was 4:45 p.m. she went back into the lounge and asked Mr. May the same question again and he shook his head and looked at her, and she looked at him. Is she upstairs, he said, saying it like it was a statement and not a question and she replied, I don't know: speaking in the same flat tone. She looked in the front room. The stereo turntable was switched on. She turned it off. The speakers clicked and the red light faded.

She went upstairs and knocked on the door of Caroline's room. There was no reply. She opened the door softly in case her daughter was sleeping but the room was empty. She went and looked in the master bedroom and then knocked on Steven's door but he was out as well. It was possible he had met up with his sister on the way home. She went back down and looked in the front room and the lounge and the kitchen again. The clock on the stove said 4:55. The clock face was rotating numbers. It had no hands.

Mrs. May remembered that she hadn't checked the bathrooms. She went and looked in the guest bathroom and then upstairs in the hallway. The en suite was as clean as she had left it except for a wrapper in the wire soap holder and milky drops of water in the basin. In the mirror her brow was creased and she was still holding the white cotton cloth, its edge dark with lamb's blood.

At 5 p.m., Mrs. May realised that neither she nor her husband had seen Caroline in the hour since they had arrived back at the house. Mrs. May checked all the rooms again and walked out to the front gate. Lights were coming on along the street. In the windows, kids were watching TV. Weekend sports ran before the news. People had stood their rubbish tins out on the sidewalk for the morning collection. Two teenage brothers were washing the car, hosing the last long worm of white detergent suds into the gutter.

Mrs. May went back into the lounge where her husband was standing now with his hands on his hips, saying nothing. He had been watching her out the window.

Ten minutes later Steven May pulled in off the road and parked his trail bike in the garage. He was still unstrapping his helmet when his parents came out and asked him where Caroline was. He didn't know. They told him to go look for her. He said he was hungry and wanted to eat first. All three of them argued about it. Steven finally left on foot, walking along the street in his motorcycle boots. He went house to house asking if Caroline was in, turning red-faced when the door was opened by one of the pretty girls his age and stammering when a parent asked him what had happened. Steven wasn't worried. His sister would turn up. This was just another drag.

Mrs. May started calling her daughter's friends. She was still on the phone when Steven returned an hour later. They argued about it again. They decided Caroline could have gone with her friends into town. Mrs. May went upstairs and looked through Caroline's wardrobe. Her daughter's warm clothes were still hanging there: the long brown coat, the jacket with the furry collar, the raincoat, even the zippered Adidas track suit top that Caroline said was warm but her mother knew wasn't adequate. Steven suggested Caroline might have borrowed something from one of her girlfriends. His mother did not reply.

Mr. May drove down to the wharf to meet the people coming off the last ferry. The wind was whistling through the tin shed. Sea spray jumped through the planking. There was one entrance to the wharf, and one exit. Mr. May stood there as the passengers walked off and on the boat. His daughter wasn't among them.

A group of young sailors were enjoying a last cigarette at the end of the jetty. They couldn't have been much older than sixteen. They had bad skin and perfectly pressed coats and they were enjoying every second until they had to walk back to the naval base. Mr. May described his daughter to them but they said they hadn't seen anyone like that around the wharf. One of the sailors asked him if something was wrong. Mr. May didn't reply.

The water was lower now. The tide had turned. The moon was out. There was more coast and nobody on it. The black rocks were sticking out of the water. The lights of the city burned inside the harbour.

Later, talking to journalists, Mr. May said he would always remember this moment. He described it as strangeness falling on the small coastal neighbourhood. The family had lived there for seventeen years and in all that time they had always felt that their children were nearby. But that night, he said, the town looked different. The streets had become wide and the water deep, and it was dark in the shadow of the head.

4.

I punched the lock on a Honda in the basement of Rory's building and dumped the bundles inside. The door remote was in the glove compartment: the ignition took less than thirty seconds. I pulled out of the car park and switched on the radio, singing to myself.

Grafton Bridge was empty. The corner shops were closed. The video store there smelled of spice. They had romances on the left-hand shelves and westerns on the right, the titles written in hand on the scratched plastic covers. It was run by the same guy who owned the other shops on the corner. He always said hello when I went in but not to me. I used a membership card I found on the sidewalk.

I drove past the hospital. The emergency doors were bright. The morgue entrance was a narrow black driveway. You'd see a police car go down there sometimes; other times a hearse.

My street was further along. The houses were black in the moonlight. Their windows were dark. I drove past with the headlights off. It was rubbish day. The trash had been set out for collection in orderly groups of three: one tall bin, one short, one bundle. The bundles were old newspapers and the short bins were bottles and cans. The groups of three notes ran all the way along the grass, as tidy as a picket fence.

I pulled over outside the brick and tile duplex at the bottom of the road and pushed my bundles out onto the grass. As I pulled away from the verge I swung the wheel hard and the car swerved, slamming the door shut under its own weight. The Honda was a crappy little ride but it felt good to be in control of something.

* * *

I dumped the car at the Pinedale Tennis Club on the side of Mt. Eden. The playing courts stood at the base of a wall created by quarrying and natural slippage. The heat trapped by the exposed volcanic rock had corrupted the colonial style plantings. An orderly line of puriri trees had spread into a giant canopy that covered the driveway. A banana palm was growing in the middle of the hydrangeas.

The courts were laid with green plastic grass. Their white grids glowed in the moonlight. They were divided by screens that disguised the rest of the grounds. If I left the car on the other side it would remain hidden until day break.

The clubhouse was shuttered. The only movement was the sound of water trickling somewhere in the rock. Everything else was still.

I parked the car with its windows down and walked out. The real grass on the path was trampled flat. The pedestrian entrance stood under the club sign. *New Members Welcome*, it said. *Novice And Experienced / Social And Competitive.*

* * *

By the time I had walked back to my place there was a sense of lightness in the sky. It wasn't quite dawn yet but it was sobering up. There was an old woman standing in the drive-way. She was wearing slippers and an old pink dressing gown. Her face was thin and her grey hair was a mess. She smiled at me, her blue eyes unblinking.

"Are you visiting Mr. Chamberlain?" she said.

"It's me, Mrs. Callaghan. It's Mark."

"I heard someone coming in and I thought, that will be Mr. Chamberlain popping round to visit. Are you on your way home from a dance?"

"That's right."

"I see you're wearing your tuxedo. So you have been at a dance?"

"Yes. Up at the Anglican Hall."

"Oh, how lovely. Were you accompanying anyone?"

"I met some friends."

"I keep waiting for the day when you bring home someone special."

"Well, not yet. But that day will come, I'm sure."

"Mr. Callaghan and I met at a gathering at the Masonic Lodge," she said. "Up in Bellevue Street. They were excellent hosts. There was punch and a band. Who was the band tonight?"

"Just a little outfit."

"I'm sorry?"

"There was a drummer and a pianist and a man playing the horn and a guy on trombone."

"A quartet."

"That's the one. You really shouldn't be coming out in the night to see what's outside, Mrs. Callaghan. It's late and you never know who could be hanging around."

"Oh, don't worry about me. When you get to my age there's not much to be scared of. I remember Mr. Callaghan was always saying I shouldn't do this or that but I'm fine, really. You can't spend every day worrying. You don't worry when you take a tram, do you?"

"Never," I said.

"Well, there you go. All the sparks and electricity above your head, but you don't worry. And I've got Dutch."

"Where is he?"

She looked around and back at me without refocussing.

"You've got me there," she said. "He's probably inside sleeping. But he'd come out if he heard someone who wasn't you. He's an excellent guard dog."

"I know he is," I said.

We were talking loud enough for the neighbours to hear but I doubted they were listening. Everyone in the street was used to the way Mrs. Callaghan shuffled around. She had been living here longer than anyone could remember—except maybe Dutch. Her unblinking stare made people think she was blind. They were half right. Mrs. Callaghan saw the people around her but not the change. She was still living in the days she remembered.

"Well, Mrs. Callaghan: I really should be getting inside."

"I didn't mean to keep you up."

"No worries. You should get back to sleep now."

"I will. God bless, Mr. Chamberlain. Please give my regards to Mrs. Chamberlain."

"I will. Good night."

She gripped the stair rail carefully in her small hands and climbed both steps to her door. I reached over and opened the insect screen. A big golden labrador was stretched out on his belly in the hall. "Hi Dutch," I said. His brow scrunched. When he saw his mistress he pushed himself up one yellow paw at a time. Arthritis made moving a big deal for both of them. Mrs. Callaghan bid me good night a second time as I shut the door.

I took a quick walk around my half of the building. The windows were closed. The scraps of paper tucked beneath the panes were still in place. I brought the bundles in from the road, carrying them one at a time in a dumb sort of effort to look casual.

I pushed the front door open with my foot. Locks are worthless. If someone like me wants to get in they will. If the cops come round they'll break it down. My place is filled with valuable things but not one of them belongs to me.

* * *

A morning chill had collected inside the hall. I undid the bundles on the old green and grey carpet and spread out all the items. It wasn't a bad grab, given the circumstances. A lot of it was small change but you need that sometimes. The leather jacket was a little big. I hung it in the wardrobe next to the CDs. My T-shirt stank of sweat. There were thirty more wrapped in a box beside the bed. I took one out of the packet and put it on.

The kitchen was clean because I never cook. The rubbish bin was packed with styrene boxes and cardboard pizza trays and trademarked paper bags. The empty cupboards smelled like sweet and sour sauce. I poured some milk into a champagne flute and stored the carton in the fridge alongside the South African-bottled Dutch beers.

The sun was coming up. A new light began to creep through the house. It broadened the hallway, picking out the items on the floor. It ran along the bookcases and the shelves. It played on the components trussed in string and plastic bags like hard quarters of meat; telephones bound in handset cables and wires; video and still cameras wrapped in bathroom towels; amplifiers muffled in sheets.

Their owners would recall that moment of sensation for years afterward: the dislocation, the disbelief, the realisation that they had been burgled. They would remember the words as they broke the news to friends or their families, their voices trembling. But beyond the moment of discovery, the fear doesn't last. People rationalise what has gone missing: after time they become almost grateful. In your imagination, there's always something worse to lose.

5.

A police car pulled up outside the Mays' house on the Sunday night that Caroline disappeared. The neighbours stood outside in groups with their hands across their faces, whispering.

The cops who responded to the call didn't look much older than the missing girl: a stocky guy with a buzz cut and a bony girl, both wearing blue uniforms that didn't fit. They listened politely to the parents' story, looking down at their notebooks when Mr. May's voice started to break. His wife was sobbing steadily, holding a handkerchief across her mouth.

Neither parent seemed to be saying anything. The two junior offices on the Sunday night shift were hard pressed to be worried about a moody teenage girl. She had probably left the house in a huff after some imaginary crisis, they thought; there was no need to worry. They made a list of her friends' names. They told Mr. and Mrs. May to stay in touch and left, a good hour before midnight. The headlights of the police car cast yellow pools on the lawn grass as it drove away.

Later that night someone called a radio station and a bulletin got put on the wire. The newspapers picked up the story for the Monday edition. By midday the family was being interviewed in their front garden. The reporters asked them for a photograph of Caroline. By the next night everyone in the country knew what she looked like but nobody could say where she was.

People rang round. Parents asked children; the children called each other up. All anyone said was that Caroline had gone. Have you seen her? Caroline May was here the other day. And now she's gone. Like she'd driven away into the night with the black and white car.

She was legally declared missing after 48 hours. The posters went up around the neighbourhood the same night. They were pasted on telephone poles and bus stops and the wharf. They were paid for by local shopkeepers. The printer who made them repeated the headline across the top and bottom of the page so the message read like a chant: *Missing Girl, Missing Girl.*

The detective in charge of the search was a man named Harry Bishop. Harry was tall and skinny with a round face and a squint. His nose was pushed slightly to one side. It showed up under the lights whenever he was interviewed for TV, which was often. The black and white screen made him look messed up and pissed off as if its confines were making him sweat. He would listen to the reporters' questions with a screwed-up face like his food had gone down the wrong way.

Harry Bishop personally interviewed Caroline's classmates at the sick room. I was third in line. He sat behind the nurse's desk scribbling notes as I talked. There was a bucket of sawdust in the corner. The apple on the desk smelled like a raincoat. When the interview was finished he sent me back with a slip of paper with the next name in the alphabet. The faces in the windows turned as I walked past.

The police set up their base of operations in the old fire station, a two-storied brick building with bamboo growing out the back. We could see the cops inside when we went by on the way home. They had installed a wall-sized pin board dedicated to everything they knew about Caroline: her clothes, height, age, weight. They had reporting systems and assigned codes and petty cash in the drawer beside the phone. They discussed their search options as they passed around the only ashtray. We saw Harry Bishop point a ruler at places on the map, the blue trails of cigarette smoke curling around him like ghosts.

* * *

They decided that if the girl had left on the ferry or driven or walked out of town she would soon be found by other police or members of the public. But if she was still in the area—if there was anything to find, in other words—she had most likely been lost around the rocks or the tunnels of North Head. Technically, there were other places she could have gone: with good luck and the right tides she could have come to grief anywhere along the shore and been washed out to sea, for instance, but the head towered above the streets like an obvious answer. It was where people looked first.

There was a strong southerly blowing on the morning of the search. Marked and unmarked police cars parked along all the roads around the point. Out on the harbour the water was scudded grey and white, the waves coming in from every direction. The clouds passed quickly, changing shapes on the ground like a spinning parasol.

The police closed the head off to the public and set up camp at the base with tents and a diesel generator. The teams were made up of uniformed cops and volunteer locals. The first group was climbing the black rocks. A policewoman in chest-high waders walked through the surf. A fisherman in a wet suit and a yellow raincoat poked a broomstick in the flax clumps growing above the tide line. The searchers looked determined but their expressions had nothing to do with what they were thinking. Their faces were stiff. Their movements were awkward.

The second team was working on an incline where the search grids had been pegged out like running tracks in white ribbon. Police in white overalls worked through each grid on their hands and knees. Photographers were hired to snap anything that might be found before it was bagged up and tagged with a corresponding number.

The scrub and the grasses were wet with rain. The ribbons shimmered in the wind. The new clouds passed over and blocked the cold spring sunlight and for a moment the shadows of the searchers disappeared.

* * *

The teams working the rocks and the grid search were stood down after sundown but the people searching the military tunnels continued into the night. The television news crews moved in lights to capture them in black and white. The gaunt, muddy faces that flashed onto the screen belonged to teachers and parents, elder brothers of classmates. The reporters pressed them for more information but they gave none. There was a rumour that this lack of information was deliberate.

There was a story going around about an upturned rowboat, and another about a tour bus that had been seen driving at sunset with a single passenger sitting near the front: a blonde girl, her face in her hands. These stories were never mentioned on the news. There was a rumour that this was deliberate, too.

Throughout the night groups of locals waited outside the tunnels with food and blankets. As the torch lights came dancing around the far end of the black corridor they prepared coffee and hot chocolate, busying themselves to hide their disappointment. The news showed the searchers gulping their hot drinks, staring ahead, saying nothing.

North Head rose up like a black fin against the stars. The cement entrances to the tunnels were dimly visible in the moonlight. Every time a search party went in to look for Caroline they marked the doors at head height with a piece of white chalk. When they exited they crossed that line with red. The idea was to prevent the searchers following in each other's tracks but the teams kept going back into the tunnels to look again anyway. When the search was finally called off the door-ways were streaked pink. The men stood on the hillside, blinking in the morning light, unable to shake the feeling that she was in there, just around the next corner, like a word on the tip of your tongue.

6.

I took the old guitar case out from under my bed and lay it open in the hallway. I tore a bath towel into strips and used them to wrap the watches, the Nikon, the cell phones and the dope before neatly arranging the bundles in the lower curves of the case, packing them in so they wouldn't bang around.

Lennox lived out in Mangere under the flight path to the airport. His house was peach-coloured with Spanish arches. The low-angled roof looked like it had been beaten down by the noise of the planes.

There was a boat and trailer on the front lawn next to a cement seal balancing a globe on its nose. The plants in the garden had dried up and the lawn was overgrown. Lennox could have paid someone to do something about that but he never did. He blamed it on the horticultural therapy.

Smoke was rising over the six foot corrugated steel fence out the back. The air was cool but the sun was already beating down. I could smell the fat on the barbecue. A Harley was chained to the rotary clothesline. The empty beer bottles were lined up inside the gate. Tui and her sisters were sitting at the plank table. Lennox's stepkids from her first marriage were banging the dog cage. I didn't recognise the other people. They all said hi.

Lennox was standing by the smoker, skinny and bow-legged in his shorts and jandals. He had the burners going full. His forehead was red and his moustache was black with sweat.

"You gonna play something for us today, Markie?" Tui said.

"Maybe."

"Lenny! You put some more on for Markie boy," Tui called out. "Put something on his bones."

"Able suggestion." Lennox poked the grill and the dripping fat made the flames shoot up. "Fuck, this thing's a bitch in the wind."

"The fella said don't put it in the open," Tui said.

"Fuck that—it's a fucking barbecue," Lennox said. He chucked her the tongs and motioned me inside.

* * *

The lounge was pink and airless. The heavy cream drapes were backed with silvery nets. The matching sofa set was pink with grey stripes. The glass top of the carved redwood Balinese coffee table was spotless. The races were playing on the wide screen TV with the sound on mute.

"It's good to see you, anyway," Lennox said. "You staying for lunch?"

"Sure thing."

"I'm gonna fix myself one. How are you going?"

"That'd be great."

He brought back two rum and cokes with plenty of ice, the condensation pricking the glass.

"Wrap yourself round that," he said.

I pushed the guitar case over to the couch and watched him

go through it. He had a businessman's reflex for talking a sale down, which was why I liked to bring around the small stuff first. He lit a cigarette before unwrapping the parcels one after the other like a bored kid at Christmas. The rum and Coke tasted sticky.

"Is this digital?" Lennox said, holding up the Nikon.

"No."

He unwrapped the cell phones.

"Are they locked?" he said.

"Default settings. 1-2-3-4."

"Good one. Nice watch."

"You reckon?"

He sniffed the dope. "You had any?"

"No."

Lennox sniffed again. He went back over everything, holding his cigarette with a crooked hand.

"Small change," he said, finally. "Not bad."

"There's some other stuff. DVDs."

"Any jewellery?"

"A couple of pieces."

"You should've brought it round today. You could have saved yourself some time."

"It was less to carry."

"For sure."

"You interested in passports, Len?"

"Have you got some?"

"Not here," I said. He wasn't even looking at me. Lennox had X-rays in the back of his head. "But I can get some."

"What country?"

"Not sure."

"If it's Asia, you bring those round," he said. "I know a guy."

"What'll he pay?"

Lennox made a face. "Depends."

He looked everything over once more before asking me how

much I wanted for the lot. I gave him a number and he said fine. He stubbed his cigarette out on the table top and shook a fresh one out of the pack.

"Mind if I have one of those?" I said.

"I thought you gave up."

"I feel like one now."

"Help yourself. Want another drink?"

"I'm fine."

"You're staying for lunch, right?"

"That'd be good."

"Is everything okay?"

"Everything's fine."

"You seem a little tense."

"Do I?"

"Yeah. Something on your mind?"

"Clear as a bell."

"Suit yourself."

Lennox leaned back on the sofa and crossed his bony legs and we sat there watching the TV for a bit. The horses were being lined up for the next race, trainers and helpers crowding each other as they led them in.

Lennox blew smoke before speaking up. "You know Hale's, right?" he said suddenly, as if the thought had just occurred to him.

"Sure," I said.

Hale's was a jewellery franchise with outlets all over the city. Mr. Hale was a little guy with grey hair and a nice smile who presented his own TV commercials like an American used car salesman. His stores sold the sort of junk teenagers buy for each other: tiny chains; gold rings shaped like a heart. *Precious things you can afford*, went the slogan. Some people sneered but a lot more got the joke and Hale's business went through the roof.

"I'm talking about the shop up on Hobson Street. You should check it out."

"What for?"

"Just take a look. See how it sits. Can you do that?"

"Sure thing."

The horses were all in the boxes now, their tails flicking behind the white metal gates. And then they were off and we were watching them, tight-lipped.

* * *

I hadn't come here to talk. Lennox knew something was up but he knew not to ask about it. It was a rule that you could follow up a disclosure but never press for one. If you steal, you learn to shut up. Knowledge is profit and liability in the outside world: you keep it to yourself.

In jail, it was different. When we were inside, talking made things cool. Lennox and I would meet up in the yard and talk every day.

Lennox did safes. What he had was a detailed knowledge of mechanisms: how to drill tumblers; how to cut; how to pull a box out of a cement floor. He knew how to use plastic and caps. He knew how to use wet towels to concentrate the blast. He could calculate the impact required to open a door as easily as he could roll his cigarettes.

Safes came in six categories. Small units were usually in the first three grades. You could open them with a hammer and chisel, peeling up a corner like the lid on a tin. The next two grades had doors that were resistant to oxyacetylene although the body could be cut or drilled. The top grade of safes were stronger and heavier. They had lead casing that made them too heavy to lift, and locks that jammed if the case was drilled, and precision doors that sealed like an oyster. The only way to open them was with a jam shot.

A jam shot was a charge exploded inside the door's hermetic seal. First you puttied the door. Then you trickled nitroglycerine between the door and the frame. And then you set it off, and the door blew itself off its own hinges. It was like judo: defeating your opponent with his own strength.

The only risk with a jam shot was setting fire to whatever was inside. Cash burned, of course: precious metal didn't. The problem nowadays was that people used safes to lock up stuff that was worthless to anyone else: documents, homemade pornography, bones, rugs, stupid paintings.

But even when there was nothing good, Lennox said, you still got a philosophical kick out of cracking a box. Before you opened it, there was nothing inside. Without you, it didn't exist.

7.

The traffic was light in town. Everyone was at work. Hale's Jewellery stood halfway along a row of ex-industrial buildings at the top of the city. The footpath was paved in lumpy asphalt. One of the parking meters had been kicked until it bent.

The awning outside Hale's sagged. The building had been an engineering workshop back in the forties. It had thick walls and a patterned steel door but the display window was unusually wide. It would have held eight panes originally, admitting enough light for the entire floor. When the premises were converted to retail it had been glazed with a single sheet. An oval frame resembling an antique picture mount had been set just inside the glass. The mount was a quick fix: an attempt to strengthen the pane.

The jewellery was displayed on white mannequins: two half-torsos and three left arms, scattered and shining with gems.

The interior of every Hale's store was the same: black walls, black display cases. There was an electric eye across the door. A bell sounded when I broke the beam. Tiny pin-lights in the ceiling made the junk in the store look like the real thing.

The serving staff wore name tags. *Introducing Dean* was broad and olive-skinned, maybe in his early twenties. His short hair was shaved to a fade. His knuckles and his earlobes were smooth. His big fingers were manicured and his suit was pressed. He was wearing a wrist chain that had been borrowed from the cabinet to demonstrate the style to customers. He had a nice smile and he was relaxed as he stood behind the women, busying himself by straightening things here and there.

Introducing Patty was small and thin with a dyed black bob that looked like something out of a 60s pop show. She had made up her face in the same heavy style that would have suited her a decade ago when it had come back in fashion for the third time. She had a small nose and a round face and deep-set eyes. Her white uniform blouse was brightened by a gold spray brooch and a touch of yellow in the lapel. The emerald on her right hand was the largest stone in the store. The wedding band was too new to be hers.

I was served by *Introducing Charlotte*, who was maybe nineteen and blinked when she smiled. One of her good teeth stood slightly forward from the others but not in a bad way. She had rolled up her sleeves and rested her hands on the counter to display the bracelets on her slender wrists. The glitter polish on her pinkie nail was chipped from picking her teeth when nobody was looking.

"Good morning, sir," Charlotte said. "Can I help you look through what we have here today?"

"I'm looking for something for my girlfriend."

"That's wonderful," she said, smiling as if I was getting it for her. "What sort of thing does your girlfriend like?"

"I'm not sure—I haven't really done this before. I'd really appreciate some advice."

"We have a whole range of pieces here. Why don't we start with some diamondesque pieces?"

"That would be great."

* * *

The Milk Barn was directly across the road from Hale's. It had secondhand furniture and a vegetarian menu and the staff and the patrons all looked the same. They were students, most of them, sitting around all day comparing homemade haircuts and holes in their label jeans. There used to be other cafés like that in the city before the business district got too expensive. The other relaxed joints had shifted to the suburbs: the Milk Barn would be the last to go.

A girl with six earrings was sitting outside at an orange plastic table smoking cigarettes and drinking spirulina. She had taken off her work boots so she could rest her bare feet on the belly of a black retriever stretched out in the sun. The dog had grey hairs on his jowls and a big belly: he looked old and tired, and happy to be there.

The first Velvet Underground album was belting out over the fake woodgrain speakers. The chalkboard menu advertised cappuccino and espresso. Next to the till was a green brandy balloon full of customers' business cards. I pocketed a few while I waited.

After a minute a guy with long black tattoos and a baseball cap that said *Elwood* shuffled over to take my order, his cuffs dragging on the lino. The tattoos on his arms were either half-finished or in the process of being burned off. The design looked like the doodles on a locker door. I ordered a latté and sat by the window.

A lot of people walk in and out of Hale's over the next hour. A sales rep with a strengthened briefcase. Three Asian girls with tiny pink backpacks. A Samoan schoolboy with a wrist chain. A woman in a beige pants suit. The staff served them at the back of the store where they disappeared into relative darkness. This simple precaution showed the staff had been trained. They didn't want anyone watching like I was doing or waiting for a grab-man.

I took the box out of my pocket. *Introducing Charlotte* was good at her job. She wouldn't let me leave without buying something. I had settled for a silver bracelet in an imitation velvet box. I took it out and draped its heavy links across my hand. The cold sent a little tingle through the scar on my thumb. It wasn't bad work as far as bracelets go. It was heavy and soft and blunt around the edges. It was made for a girl.

I put it back in my pocket with the passports. I turned to look around the café. The windows along the side of the Milk Barn were barred but the lock on the front door was old. The kitchen and the rest rooms were at the far end. An alley ran down the back of the building. I couldn't see any sign of an alarm.

Elwood must have seen me looking round and remembered about my coffee. He apologised for being so slow when he bought it over. I said didn't mind. Both of us had other things on our minds.

8.

The windows of Stillaman Rush were filled with passing clouds. The single tower had been built with eight sides. A window seat at the law firm was a sign of prestige: the extra walls allowed the firm to employ twice as many vital people. The foyer was transparent. The air conditioning was a little sharper than the world outside.

The security guard looked up when I walked in. His name tag said Mr. Whelan. He was in his late sixties and his belly was stretching his zippered uniform jacket. His hair was dyed dark brown.

I showed him the bracelet. He didn't blink.

"This belongs to someone who works here," I said. "Josie someone."

"What's her last name?" Mr. Whelan said.

"I only know her first name. She was playing pool with some of her friends up at a place on Ponsonby Road. I was talking to her and she dropped this. She left it behind."

"Josie."

"Josie. She said she was a clerk here."

"A clerk at Stillaman Rush?"

"Yes."

"And her name's Josie, and this item is hers?" he said.

"That's the one."

"And you're a friend of hers?"

"I was just talking to her at the bar."

Mr. Whelan took the chain and turned it in his dry hand. He was looking for hallmarks but there weren't any: he could tell it wasn't solid silver just by looking at it. He kept hold of it as he ran his finger down the phone list.

"So you don't know her last name?" he said. Making me repeat everything: definitely an ex-cop.

"It might have been Richmond, I think. Blonde, about so tall."

He squinted at me like the air-conditioning was blowing cold. Security guards have led long lives but now and then you get one who knows what he's doing.

"Okay," he said. "I can track her down. What's your name and contact number?"

"I don't think she'll even remember me. I just wanted to give her the bracelet back. I'm really just doing this as a favour to the barman."

"And what's his name?" he said.

I had already turned towards the door.

"I'm double parked, mate," I said. "You're after Josie Richmond."

I walked out onto the street wiping my hands on my shirt.

* * *

My hands got sweaty when I talked about her to people. I didn't know why that was. I could picture her dressed for work in the same white shirt and navy jacket as the other clerks in the firm. It was practically a uniform. The other girls were the same age as Josie but they seemed older when they were all gussied up.

The women were thinner than their natural weight. They didn't smoke because they didn't want to smell of cigarettes. They skipped meals because they didn't want to get fat and lived off coffee so they could work longer hours. And they wanted to find out about me, Josie said, because I was different. I knew she would never tell them.

I looked back at Mr. Whelan standing in the big transparent foyer. The shining horizon carried a hint of pink across the windows.

Above him people were walking between the desks; typing; putting things in files. Looking up from street level, the first things that caught your eye were the ceiling tiles and the harsh fluorescent lights. But looking out from the office at night the interior was reflected endlessly, running across the skyline like a misted garden of desks and cubicles. You were duplicated,

too, by the angled windows: rows and rows of yourself standing high above the street.

I framed the facade with my hands so it looked as if it were
speeding across the sky. It would be dark before anyone from
the firm went home. There's so much competition, Josie told
me: nobody wants to be the first to leave.

I thought picture her sitting in her cubicle, now, up on the
fifth level. The wall dividers were elbow high and grey. Inside
her space were two desks and two adjustable chairs positioned
to face away from each other.

The desks were dressed with similar items arranged in
roughly the same order: pens, staplers, coloured sticky notes
hanging off the computer monitor. The zippered plastic purse
in her desk drawer held aspirin and sanitary pads. There was a
short rolled umbrella, paper towels, roll-on deodorant that
smelled faintly like her.

A pair of earrings were lying with the paper clips in the sta-
tionery tray: plain gold studs on a card, the sort of thing you buy
for a few dollars in a shopping mall. Her unworn running shoes
were in a plastic bag.

There was an internal directory pinned up on the divider. It
listed staff alphabetically with no indication of gender. It was
strange to read her last name shouted in capitals and her first in
italics, like an afterthought. Josie hadn't written my name on
anything near the phone. My number wasn't on speed dial. She
had memorised it. And so the one thing in her cubicle that gave
me a good feeling about her was the one thing I couldn't find.

I had never told Josie that I had stood inside her office. It
had been so easy. Stillaman Rush contracted three different
firms of overnight cleaners to maintain the building. All I had
to do for the supervisor to accept me as casual staff was turn up
for the shift with a pair of white overalls and a stupid look on
my face. I flicked him a fake ID and he gave me a squeegee bottle and a bucket of rags and sent me up to clean the windows.

When I had finished looking through Josie's things I spent the rest of the night tidying the place up. The main offices were protected by blinds which were never raised, judging from the dust. I went through some of the desks but didn't find anything worth much. Besides, taking anything would get the others into trouble and I didn't want to do that. They were nice people: a family business, with most of them over from the Islands. The supervisor was shorter than me and twice my weight. When we broke for lunch at midnight he saw I had nothing to eat and gave me one of his sandwiches. His knuckles were seared with blonde scars like he had pressed them on a griddle. On his waist was a wire hoop with maybe fifty keys on it, different cuts of brass and silver worn by locks all over the city. You couldn't put a price on a collection like that.

9.

Lennox knocked on my kitchen window around midday. He was dressed for work: patent leather shoes, grey slacks, open-neck shirt, neck chain. When I looked out Mrs. Callaghan was talking to him in her determined way. She was still in her dressing gown, clutching the rail outside her door as if the steps were about to give out from under her. I pulled my jeans on and went outside.

"You have a visitor, Mr. Chamberlain," she said, turning to me.

"Thanks, Mrs. Callaghan."

"I thought you'd already left for work."

"I'm just home for lunch."

"Mr. Chamberlain has been working the night shift," she said.

"Is that right?" Lennox said.

"I've known him since he was a little boy."

"That's the story."

"You're welcome to come in for some tea."

"Not for me, thanks."

"Well, I won't keep you two men from your work, then," she said. She opened the fly screen and then her door. She turned back as she closed the screen and waved very slowly. Lennox waved back, his gold ID bracelet catching the bright sun. The bracelet had been a present from Tui. The initials on the tag were CLF—her ex-husband's.

* * *

"Lovely woman," Lennox said.

"Give it a rest."

"Says she's got a dog."

"Dutch. He's older than her."

"No worries there, then. And she's always been here?"

"I think so."

"What's this place worth nowadays?"

"No idea."

"Must be a bit."

"Like I said."

"Have I come at a bad time? I was just seeing a mate in town."

"Sure thing."

"I can wait if you want to get dressed."

"I am dressed."

He laughed. "Good for you."

"You want a coffee?"

"Milk and one."

"I remember."

"You can come in, if you want."

"I'm fine out here, mate. Don't you worry."

Lennox didn't want to see what I had inside. He sat down on the step and lit a cigarette. I made us two cups of instant and brought them outside. He lit a second cigarette and passed it over. I leaned back to let the sun warm my stomach. Lennox hunched forward balancing his forearms on his knees. There was no sign of Mrs. Callaghan or her dog. The street at the end of the driveway was empty. Lennox drew in a lungful of smoke, squinting.

"So you checked out Hale's," he said, as if he already knew.

"Sure did."

"What'd you reckon?"

"Bit of a shambles. I'm surprised he can get insurance for it. The front window's too big. There are no automatic barriers. The high-priced items are displayed alongside the cheap goods, which is going to make an audit impossible. People wander in and out. It's on a main street. Dean looks like a strong guy but he's stuck behind the counter in a nice tight suit. I don't see him running after anyone."

"Ha," Lennox cackled. "Did you see the cameras?"

"Everyone's got cameras. They never show anything. All you see is some blurry guy on the TV."

"And yet, there it is," Lennox said. "A big gaping hole, like you said."

I shrugged. "Maybe he's busy. Maybe his security firm's no good."

"Maybe."

Lennox waited. I swilled my coffee around in the mug.

"It's an inside job," I said.

"For the insurance," Lennox nodded. "We remove some items, Mr. Hale sends in a claim. I sell the material back to Mr. Hale for cost; he on-sells the pieces through his own stores in Wellington and Sydney—the one retail chain the police won't be watching. It's easy and it's guaranteed."

"So how do we do it?"

"Smash and grab."

"You're joking."

"Not at all," he said. "That's the beauty of it. It's all set up. The quality items are going to be left out on display in the window instead of being put away in the safe. All you need to do is break the window, grab it and walk away. Hale tells the cops someone left it out by mistake."

"Who, on the staff?"

"You saw them. You tell me."

I considered it.

"Dean's straight," I said. "No Borstal scars. He looks like he's married and goes to church on Sundays. But maybe his wife gambles. Maybe they pay tithes. Maybe they've borrowed. If you gave him a moral excuse, he'd be up for it."

"There's Patty."

"She was probably the first person Mr. Hale hired, so he could trust her. But she's too experienced to make a mistake like leaving the good jewellery out. Charlotte isn't too bright. You could trick her into doing it, maybe."

Lennox was using his fingernail to pick at something between his front teeth.

"So what do you reckon?" he said.

"It's all of them."

"Good for you." He got whatever it was out from his teeth and flicked it away. "Nine months ago a nice gentleman from Canberra offered Mr. Hale a pension investment scheme. Hale sold it to half his staff. All the shop girls and store managers signed away their pension payments and personal savings in return for a twenty percent interest rate over six years."

"And it was a scam."

"Total scam. Money's gone: Hale has to refinance. Dean, Patty and Charlotte will get a little extra for leaving the jewels out and sharing the blame."

"For a smash and grab," I said. "It still sounds kind of amateur."

"That's how it's meant to look. That's the whole point."

"Right."

The instant coffee was pretty bad. Lennox had nearly finished his. I stared down the driveway, turning the cup between my palms.

"Is there a problem?" Lennox said. He knew there was a problem. When someone offered you a job you either took it or said no. Thinking too hard or asking too many questions was a sign of mistrust.

"There's no problem," I said.

"You don't seem too happy."

"I'm alright."

"You're sure."

"I bumped into someone the other night."

"While you were working?"

"More or less. You must have had it happen."

"Not with safes, mate. Once you've pulled the fucker out of the wall you're done. There's nothing to go back for."

"I go back all the time. People buy new stuff but they never change the windows and alarms. After you've gone in once, you can go back anytime. It's the nature of the work."

"Exactly. It's a totally fucking different business." He watched his smoke drift upwards. "So it rattled your cage."

"A bit."

"You'll work it out." He stubbed his cigarette out on the stone and lit another. "It happens, to be honest with you. It's a small country. Stick around and you get caught. And you don't want that, right?"

"No."

"When'd you last take a holiday?"

"Not for ages."

"Take a break. Get out of town. Friend of mine's got a place up north. Chuck half a beast in the freezer and go fishing for your tea and lay low."

"Sounds good."

"I mean it," he said. "You're not getting any younger. When we were inside that was, what—your fifth bust?"

"Something like that."

"See, right now—in the eyes of the law—you're rehabilitated. You were a troubled youth, you fell in with a bad crowd, you learned your lesson, and now you're on the straight and up. But if the cops come here tomorrow," Lennox hooked his thumb at the back door. "What are they gonna find?"

"The cops aren't coming."

"Just say they did."

I didn't reply.

"You'd get hammered," Lennox said. "Hoarding stolen property. For the purpose of dealing in stolen property. These actions will demonstrate before a judge and jury that you have not been discouraged from the criminal life. That previous remedies have not worked. That a stronger sentence is called for."

"You should be a lawyer."

"I've heard it all, mate. I know it by heart. If they arrest you now, you'll go down for a long time: three, four, five years—just at the moment when you realise how little time you really have left. I'm not shitting you."

"So you're saying I shouldn't do Hale's?"

"I'm just saying, know when to leave."

I stared at the end of the driveway. I had enough inside to live off for a year if I wanted to lie low, but I didn't feel like lying low. I wasn't going to sit around waiting for permission.

"It's a window," I said. "It'll break."

"Good man. Just watch yourself."

"I know what I'm doing."

"Sweet."

10.

Josie called from the office, late. She sounded bright on the phone. She didn't care if she was talking within earshot of someone else. If anything, someone listening made it better. And her voice changed when she was talking to me on the phone. She'd go from being Miss Richmond Speaking to Josie just like that: as if someone had thrown a switch.

"Thank you for the bracelet," she said.

"How did you know it was me?"

"It was anonymous. You should have said you were there—I would have come down."

"You would have been busy."

"It was very sweet of you."

"Do you like it?"

"Yeah, totally," she said. "You should have come up, just to say hello. I could have introduced you to some of the people on my floor."

I couldn't imagine what that would be like. I didn't feel like running the gauntlet of her work friends.

"I had to go to a meeting," I said. "So the bracelet was a surprise?"

"It was."

"And you really like it?"

"Sure."

I wondered if she did. She had a lot of jewellery.

"So what was your meeting about?" she said.

"I had to see a man about a dog."

"What sort of dog?"

"I'll tell you later. You're working late."

"Mr. Stillaman has a big client presentation tomorrow. And we're collating some figures for an internal insurance assessment."

"Who's 'we'?"

"You know, us. The girls." Her voice was smiling now.

"How's Mr. Stillaman?"

"He's really hot."

"Okay."

"I think about him all the time."

"Okay."

"Sometimes I touch myself."

"I'm just making conversation."

"You don't have to. You can just talk."

"I'm not so good at talking."

"Tell me what you've been doing?"

"Sleeping in."

"And?"

"And that's about it. There's nothing else to do. You're at work."

"This is a work-related call. You're a valued client."

"Who sent you a bracelet."

"It's been known to happen," she said. "Why don't you want to see me?"

"I do want to see you."

"Then come out," she said. "Tonight."

* * *

Josie's friend was playing at Miller's Cave: which friend, she didn't say. The Cave was downstairs in a warehouse up by the university. The sign on the door said Happy Hour started at 6 p.m. and never stopped. The 7 p.m. part had probably been wiped off by a patron but you couldn't be a hundred per cent sure.

The band was going hard out inside. The room smelled of hops and sweat and cleaning fluid, and the air above people's heads was grey. It was mostly a student crowd, cheering whenever the band stopped and starting up again in the middle of a song. Josie said she wanted to go up front so I waited for her at the bar. There were some old guys drinking there with their backs to the noise, hunched and white-faced. The kids had a lot to learn.

We had got there in time for the band's final set. They ran out the last number for a good two or three minutes trying to see who could sustain the last note. It was a relief when the drummer wrapped it up and the lights came on. I could see Josie in the crowd, waving her arms around.

Afterwards we went downtown and bought a hamburger at the White Lady. The White Lady was a kerbside diner that parked at the bottom of Shortland Street every weekend. A tractor towed it into the space on Friday night and out again on Monday morning. In between the operators served what seemed like every clubber and passerby in a two mile radius. The fry cook with the grey short back and sides had repaired the bridge of his spectacles with sticking plaster. The cook with the spider web on his neck noticed my knuckles but said nothing.

I ordered a cheeseburger with egg and Josie ordered a corn toasted sandwich. It was cold waiting on the sidewalk. She had worked up a sweat in Miller's Cave and was shivering now in her thin office clothes.

"You should have changed," I said.

"I didn't want to go home."

I gave her my leather jacket to wear. She pulled it on over her blazer. She looked good in it in the way girls always do. The sleeves hung over her hands. When her sandwich came she held the paper bag with her fingertips so the butter fat didn't drip on the leather. She ate daintily and I wolfed it down. The other customers waiting were watching us with the same expression Rory Jones had on his face. But they didn't know what I knew about her. Josie didn't wash her feet. She swore when she was drunk. She banged her fist on the table to make a point. She gazed at the pavement when she walked by herself. She was in danger of developing a slouch.

She wiped her hands on the bag and tossed at the bin and missed. "This thing's so damn heavy," she said, tugging at the black leather jacket. "I can hardly lift my arms. How do you wear it all the time?"

"I never noticed."

I watched as she unzipped the breast pocket and zipped it up again. I was reminded of something. Before I could say it, she had felt inside and found the passports. She pulled one out and saw what it was.

"Are you going somewhere?" she said. And then she opened it and saw Rory Jones's photograph. I said nothing. She put it back in the pocket and took out one of the Indonesian passports and read the name inside.

"I can't even pronounce this," she said.

"I can't, either."

"You could sell these for a lot of money," she said. "Passports are big business, now."

I didn't say anything.

"Do you want the jacket back?"

"No. You look good in it." I wiped my nose. "I found those."

"I know you did."

The ventilator on the side of the diner was rattling. The fan was off its bearings, squeaking into the night. In the daytime the reflections from the office windows filled the corner with sun but the only light now was the servery's halo reaching out in the darkness. Josie zipped my jacket up to her neck and stuck her hands in the pockets and rocked back on her heels for a bit, jiggling. A taxi pulled into the stand across the street. Some people climbed out, slamming the doors and shouting. You couldn't tell if they were drunk or happy or angry. They were just making noise.

"I have to deliver some documents later this week," Josie said. "It's a long drive. Would you like to come?"

"I don't have a car."

"They're lending me one."

"They do that?"

"If you're a girl, sure. If they gave it to one of the guys they'd just thrash it. Hand-brakes and stuff."

"That'd be cool," I said.

"So you really want to come?"

"You asked me: I said yes."

"I'm a lucky girl."

11.

I was nervous about doing Hale's, despite what I'd said to Lennox. Breaking a shop window on an empty street late at night would be like sending up a signal flare. Smash and grab works best in a crowd. The more people who witness an event, the greater the confusion, the easier it is to get away. A lone witness is more likely to be accurate and give chase: a group of people will hold each other back. I've read studies on it.

To do the job right, I needed a lift. A driver parked just around the corner wouldn't see what I was doing. The guy didn't need to be smart, or even trustworthy. I went looking for Daisy.

* * *

The sun was falling at the top of K Road. The sky behind the gas station was orange. The awning lights were blinking into artificial life, flooding the pump lanes with shimmering blue and white. The taxis were just coming onto the rank for their shift, parking up for the hour or so before the dinner crowds started calling.

I saw Daisy's bronze Holden parked at the end of the rank. He could stay there all night and still make money. When he wasn't driving fares the long way home or short-changing immigrants Daisy sold glue and spray paint to street kids who'd been banned from the local hardware stores. Sometimes Daisy charged an extra twenty cents for the plastic bag the solvents had come in; other times he let them have it for free, as a favour.

Daisy was reading *Hollywood Week*, blowing cigarette smoke over the pictures spread out on the steering wheel. There was a yellow vial of air freshener fixed on the dashboard and a pair of baby's booties dangling from the rearview mirror. The driver's seat was draped with wooden massaging beads that pressed into his flesh.

Daisy was big. He wore thick-lensed spectacles that shrank his eyes and made his face look bigger. His wiry black hair was pinned back with a bone comb and he spoke in a high, sweet voice, like a girl's. His wife was also a taxi driver. When he brought the car home at the end of his shift she'd take it out on hers. It was Mrs. Daisy who thought up the solvent business, apparently. They lived in Mount Roskill and had three kids— happy and healthy, so the story went.

I climbed in the back seat. Daisy fixed me in the mirror with his blind man's stare.

"How's it going?" I said.

"You're a good looking one," he said, not blinking.

"Are you keeping busy? Are you on shift tonight?"

"That's right. It's gonna get pretty busy later I reckon."

"You reckon?"

"Yeah. It's quiet now but it's going to get pretty crowded."

"Listen, Daisy—I want to book a cab for later to pick me up."

"You can book me, sweetie," he said, his tongue rolling round in his mouth.

"Up on Wyndham Street at midnight. Can you pick me up there?"

"Yeah, I can probably do that."

"I really need to know that you're going to be there."

"Willis Street."

"Wyndham Street," I corrected him. "Just around the corner."

"Yeah, I know where that is."

"Wyndham Street at midnight."

"How many people are you wanting—because I can get you a van, if you want," he said. "It's just a bit extra for a van, but."

"I don't need a van. I just need you to be in Wyndham Street at midnight."

"Okay," he said. "Well, I should be able to do that, if I'm not too busy. Some nights it gets busy, you know, and all the drivers are picking people up."

"I'm going to book you," I said. "I've got some money I'll give you now." I took out a twenty dollar bill. "I'll give you twenty now, and another twenty plus the fare when you pick me up on Wyndham Street at midnight."

"Yeah, I know where that is," he said.

I held up the twenty and he reached around to take it, the cover of wooden beads clicking as he turned.

"So see you at midnight, okay?" I said.

"What's a good-looking fella like you up to, then?"

"I've got a date and I don't want to be late for it. It's really important. So I'll see you then, okay?"

"I can probably do it."

"See you at midnight," I said. I repeated the place and time again as I got out but he had already gone back to reading *Hollywood Week*, the flashgun smiles spread across his lap.

* * *

The last thing keeping the Milk Barn open was a scuffed rubber wedge. The duty manager was sitting out front in a brown T-shirt that said *Porn Star*. She was smoking a rollie: her friends were drinking beers. They all looked sideways at me as I entered, pissed off that I was interrupting the staff meeting. I stood at the counter and read the blackboard menu until the Porn Star got the message that I wasn't going to leave. She walked around to the other side of the till and turned *After the Gold Rush* up a notch.

"The kitchen's closed," she said. "And we'll be closing soon."

"I'll have a Shiraz, thanks."

She wrote the word *wine* on a pad by the till.

"Where will you be sitting?" she said.

I looked around at the empty room.

"Over there, at the back."

"I'll bring that to you," she said, writing down the table number in huge loopy handwriting.

The dope smell wasn't as obvious at the other end of the room. I went into the men's. The window above the toilet cistern opened onto the alley that ran along the back of the building. The window shut on a brass latch. I unscrewed it but left it in place so it appeared secure, at least to someone who was stoned.

When I came out I found a glass of white wine waiting for me on the wrong table. The girls had gone back to their conversation. There was a story in the paper about the break-ins at Rory's place: *Developer Victim of Burglary*. As if that mattered.

I glanced up at the Porn Star now and then. I didn't resent her wanting to take the night off. Hospitality is shitty work. They were just smoking and having a good time. Back on K Road, Daisy was probably chasing the same thing, sitting around and getting along. Across the road in the window of

Hale's the stones that shouldn't have been there were gleaming under the lights.

* * *

I waited up the road while the Porn Star locked up. She linked arms with her friends and all three of them headed off to wherever. I walked down the back alley and located the window of the men's. It opened like a book. I lifted myself up and crawled inside.

The white walls radiated a neutral, almost imaginary luminescence. The urinal smelled of those briguettes that are meant to disguise the smell but only make it worse. My stomach turned and then settled again. I screwed the window latch back in place, just to make things interesting.

The silent café smelled of beans and burned oil. The ants were already moving across the kitchen floor. A grey cube of rat poison had rolled into the corner. I went through the shelves and found a set of dishwashing gloves, a squirt bottle of manuka honey and the corked Shiraz.

I let myself out the front door and stood outside. It was just on midnight. The air was warm. I could see two people at the bus stop further up the road. Their ride was at least an hour away. I checked my watch. I checked left and right. All the other premises were closed. A car ran the red light at the intersection and disappeared. The street slipped back into limbo.

I crossed the road.

The alarm speaker outside Hale's was an old-fashioned bullhorn. I squeezed the honey into the cone, filling it until it dripped down my wrists. Then I picked up the Shiraz and swung it at the glass like an Indian club.

The bottle punched straight through the plate glass and exploded into the display shelves in a pink bloom of foam. The alarm yelped, coughed and gagged, squeaking on the honey. A second alarm sounded inside the store.

The guys at the bus stop stood up to watch. The bottle had punched a hole like a rock through a car windscreen but the cracks wouldn't budge. I stepped back and kicked. It took a hell of a lot more work than I thought it would.

The bus stop men shouted. I reached inside and stripped the mannequins. I shook the rings off the white plastic arms and stuffed them in my pockets. The bus stop men were coming towards me now. I scooped up the rest and started to run.

I was sprinting when I came around the corner but I still had enough breath to cheer when I saw the bronze Holden. Daisy had parked it sticking out from the sidewalk at a crazy angle, his nerveless hand dangling a cigarette out the window. I jumped in the back. A Tammy Wynette song was wandering across the radio. The dispatcher was barking on the CB.

Daisy regarded me for an awfully long time.

"You're a good looking one," he said.

"Just get going, yeah?"

"Where're you off to tonight, then?"

"Let's get going, man." I looked back over my shoulder.

"It's quiet now," Daisy said, rolling the words around his mouth like marbles. "But it's going to get pretty crowded later on, I reckon."

I stared at him in the driver's mirror. He stared right back. He had understood me enough to turn up and that there was money in it and that he could probably squeeze me for a little more, but another part of his brain couldn't process the urgency of the situation. Daisy had been loaded so many hours of the day for so long that there was no real difference between waking and sleeping for him now, between thinking and not thinking.

The shouts were getting louder. I was wet with sweat. We needed to get away fast. I reached over and grabbed his fat soft shoulder.

"Daisy? You're with me, man. You'll be in the shit."

"It's none of my business, fella."

"I'll say it's you and you can never prove it."

Daisy blinked, cottoning on. He stamped on the accelerator and the taxi shot forward.

He didn't switch his lights on until we were two blocks away, weaving some weird evasive route of his own imagining. I made him drop me a good distance from my place and hid in some bushes just off the street. I had to wait a long time before he drove off.

Mrs. Callaghan's TV was shimmering in the front room when I got home. I did the usual circuit of the house to check that everything was okay. And then I stopped, because it wasn't.

The lounge window was wide open. The paper ticket that had been tucked into the crack was now lying on the ground outside.

I walked back up to the end of the drive. The other houses were still. The empty cars were parked along the street. The trees were dark thoughts.

I walked back to my own front door.

And knocked.

Nobody answered. I pushed the door open with my foot. Nothing moved. I took a deep breath and went inside. There was no sound. I could feel the fresh air blowing in from the other room. I went through the place quietly, checking around each corner in the darkness. Everything was in place. The lounge was the same as I'd left it. I watched the folds of the curtains roll gently in the breeze. It made no sense. Why would someone would walk up to the window and open it and then walk away?

I saw it when I flicked on the lights. It was in the middle of the floor. A paper aeroplane.

I grasped the corners of the wings and unfolded it. The

poster had faded over time but the letters were still easy to read. *Missing Girl*, it said. *Missing Girl*.

12.

The photograph in the Missing Girl poster showed Caroline standing in the dappled sunlight, laughing at whoever was holding the camera. The police used the same photograph for the TV, and the newspapers ran it all the time. Nobody knew where the photograph of Caroline had come from but it became the only way people saw her from then on. It was how she would look forever.

A boy travelling back to the city on the Sunday night ferry said he saw Caroline standing on the unlit bow. She was wearing jeans and a man's raincoat, but barefoot in the cold. Police appealed to everyone who had been on that ferry to come forward. Five, including a ticket collector, recalled a girl standing in the bow. Two of them said she'd had short hair. A third said her hair was dark brown and she'd been wearing a leather jacket.

The ticket collector said he'd seen the girl come on board with an older man in a business suit and that she was much younger than Caroline May: more like eight or nine. A father and daughter were later identified as the man and the girl and the report was eventually discounted. The boy, however, insisted it was Caroline who he had seen standing in the ferry bow. She had bloody knuckles and bare feet and she was singing to herself in a soft voice. The only thing he couldn't remember was the song.

A retired couple driving past the local cemetery saw a blonde girl standing outside the gates. The police issued a statement appealing for other eyewitnesses to come forward. None did. In a television interview the couple speculated that they had seen Caroline's ghost or spirit. Police searched the cemetery and two fresh plots were re-opened but the only dead people they found were the ones who were supposed to be there.

Caroline's brother Steven was questioned repeatedly about his sister's disappearance. The interview was routine but the locals became suspicious. Steven's crowd wore narrow-shouldered denim jackets and cowboy buckles and homemade tattoos. They drove down Queen Street on Friday nights and raced other cars at the lights. They liked Motörhead and Led Zep and Lizzy.

The so-called gang was little more than a nuisance but now their image hardened in people's minds. Their games started to look real. The local cops broke up the parties and impounded one of the cars. The boys protested. They told reporters they meant no harm. They were just being themselves, but that wasn't enough anymore, and none of them was smart enough to work it out.

* * *

Detective Harry Bishop's team posed a mannequin in the shopping arcade and dressed it in new, clean elephant bells with patterns stitched around the cuffs. They buttoned its white blouse higher than Caroline usually wore it so that she would not appear immodest. They fitted it with a blonde wig that was accurate to how all the girls remembered Caroline's hair to be, but was in fact longer and straighter and more perfect than it ever was.

The mannequin itself was new, with a white face and blank eyes and a smile. The police stood it in front of a folding display of photographs, the Missing Girl posters. The dummy stood in the arcade for a week, then the local library, then the ferry terminal. The blouse softened to off-white. The wig curled in the salt air.

The police set up a free number for people to call if they had any information about the missing girl. There was a rumour that if callers hook-flashed five times—the number of letters in *Carol*—the machine would play back all the messages previous callers had left. There was a rumour that one of the callers had played a recording of the Beach Boys song *Caroline No* into the phone, the voices echoing down the line.

Later the mannequin was removed for cleaning. Someone washed the clothes and combed the wig and returned it to the arcade: who exactly, we didn't know.

* * *

The tunnels on North Head were re-opened after the police took down the grids. Locals started to mount their own searches. They lined up outside the fire station to make reports or hand in things that were important. The constable on the front desk had a routine for weeding out the lamest ones. Here is a piece of paper, she would say, tapping her menthols into the tennis ball can. Write down your name and contact details. Write down what you know. Most people would hand the form back with nothing on it. People came in once a week. One old woman came in every day just to say hello.

All documents were numbered according to the big map downstairs before being copied in triplicate, indexed and stored. The photocopier dripped carbon on the floor like spoor. The shelves became stacked with box files.

Three weeks into the investigation, the cops found something was eating the files. Harry sent the constable from the front desk to get mousetraps. She bought them at the local store and the news spread like wildfire: the cops can't even catch mice.

A taxi driver saw a blonde girl sitting between a driver and a male passenger in a black Holden, late at night. The Holden was splattered with mud and all three passengers were wearing sunglasses. The police searched the motor vehicle register. They cross-referenced owners' names with criminal records. They searched sites where a vehicle might have been abandoned. They checked secondhand dealers and wrecker's yards.

A local panel beater, Tony Lambert, owned a dark green Holden. The police questioned him. They searched the car. They took hair and dust samples from the interior. They brushed the machine for fingerprints. They photographed the tyre treads and the bonnet, the bed. When the samples came back from the laboratory the results showed no blood in the car. The soil was from Tony's front lawn. The hair and skin belonged to Tony and his dog. The fingerprints were Tony's. He could account for his movements on the Sunday night, which he'd spent with his long-term girlfriend, a teller at the local bank.

The police took Tony's name off the list. But people who saw him driving the Holden continued to report it. Tony started parking his car at home during the day. Then the Holden was vandalised while he was at work. First the tyres were slashed. Then a door was kicked in. One day Tony arrived home to find the word *killer* scratched on the bonnet. He was so pissed off he drove it to the local tip, threw the keys after it and started walking home.

A dozer operator saw him abandon the car and called the cops. Five minutes down the road, Tony was picked up by a squad car and held at the local police station until Harry Bishop himself went over and confirmed who the man was. He found Tony Lambert handcuffed in a chair and swearing at everyone in the room, his eyes red, his face crumpled with compromised anger and guilt. Yes, Harry Bishop said: that's not the man we're looking for.

* * *

Harry Bishop came round to my house to interview me a second time. My mother answered the door in her checkout uniform with a cigarette in her hand.

"So is there a Mr. Chamberlain around?" he asked.

"Not for a while," she said, and showed him inside. Harry pointed his finger at my *Hang Ten* T-shirt when he saw it.

"*Hang Ten*," he said. "You surf?"

"He doesn't swim," my mother said.

"I can swim," I told him. "I just don't like the ocean."

Harry sat forward in the dining room chair, his hands clasped between his knees. "I know about teenagers," he said. "You keep secrets. You never say what really matters. You never write down names."

He sat and waited, acting casual.

I told him I knew Caroline from class. She was friends with Varina Sumich. I didn't know what she did that weekend. I hadn't heard her talking about it. She hadn't said anything to anyone.

My mother closed it down after an hour because she had to go to work. She told Harry he could come back and talk to me as long as she was there. And then she went to get her keys and Harry got a precious minute to lean in close and say: 'Listen. Is there anything else—anything? We won't say anything to your mother. Just between you and me: is there anything I need to know?"

I squinted into the distance. Harry leaned forward. And then I just sucked it back again and shook my head.

Later I went and hid in the bamboo bushes behind the fire station and watched Harry Bishop sitting at his desk. The extractor fan outside his window was broken. The tangled switch cords were attracting cobwebs and dust. The sticker on the side of the fan casing said *Protect the Environment*. Harry kept the files stacked on his desk one on top of the other until they made a wall between him and the rest of the office. When he shouted at someone on the phone it was like a gun going off: *brat brat brat*. He would take a swig of vodka and then gulp his coffee and then take another swig of vodka. He was out of breath from walking around and shouting at people. You could tell he was angry that someone had gone missing in such a small country. You could tell his day was passing in gasps.

13.

Missing Girl: Missing Girl. The poster in my hands was old. The paper was new. I raised it to the light and saw a tiny black triangle where the original had been pressed against the scanner platen. It was a photocopy. But it was real. Whoever had folded it into a paper plane and flown it through the window would have seen everything lying inside: the TVs, the appliances, the wall-to-wall stolen goods. The poster something else now. It said someone had found me. It said they knew who I was, what I did, where I'd come from.

I peered out at the driveway. I tried to remember the vehicles I'd seen parked up on the street. I hadn't seen any strangers around. Someone could be watching me now. But why watch, if they knew everything already?

Maybe they were expecting me to come after them. Maybe they were going to come back.

I was two steps behind. I had to sit it out. I had to be prepared—but for what?

Missing girl.

The window was still open. The breeze brought the curtains to life.

The best window job I ever did was a travel agent's in Mission Bay. It was a Sunday night. The silver alarm tape running around the edge of the window was shining in the street lights. I dug a jimmy under the lip of the sill and jumped up and brought all my weight down on it hard and the window cracked open and the alarm went off. The noise masked the screech of wood as I jerked it open. I jumped inside, ran to the grey filing cabinet by the fax machine and stabbed it with the jimmy and wrenched, pulling it open. The cash drawer was inside. I dropped the bar and stuffed the bills in my pocket and rolled back out the window. I had been inside less than 30 seconds. I put the bills in my pocket and walked slowly back along the waterfront, under the trees.

It took a long time before anyone came out and looked around. People thought it was a fire alarm. I just kept walking, glancing back over my shoulder now and then like any other concerned citizen. Nearly six hundred dollars. It was that easy. Because people are that stupid.

The hinge on the lounge window barked when I closed it. My stomach ached.

* * *

I dumped the jewellery in the kitchen sink. I rinsed off the splinters and the stink of wine. I wrapped the jewels in a cloth, a bundle the size of an apple. Instinctively I wanted to hide it but there was no point. Everything around me was stolen.

I had another beer. I took a shower. My hands were covered in shallow cuts. I dabbed the skin with disinfectant. I checked myself in the mirror, running my fingers through my hair. Hair is important in police sketches. Witnesses remember moustaches, beards, the way eyebrows are shaped.

I found a pair of nail scissors in the bathroom cabinet and started to cut it, snicking off chunks with the curved blades.

The first pass was rough. The wet hanks stuck to my lips. I brushed them off. They spread on the floor. They fell down my neck. I bent forward and felt my way along my neck, measuring the cutting length with my fingers. I stuck myself a couple of times, but I got it pretty even.

I found an old electric razor. The teeth were gummed but it still worked. I ran it over my skull. I blew the brown teeth clean and the clippings danced in the yellow light. When I looked back in the mirror my face was smaller and younger and my shoulders were broad. I swept up the hair and put it in the trash. I washed the bristles out of my cuts.

I got another beer and sat out on the step, in the dark.

The back yard was quiet. It was good to have something growing out there. The neighbouring villas stood so close together the night smelled like warm cement. The garden looked like an architect's drawing when it was first put in. The plants were spiky and alien and the ground was scattered with wood chips. But over the years clover had sprouted between the cover and the spiked grasses had spread until they died in the center and the pretty seedlings that looked like office plants had erupted into trees. Now it just looked like a mess, but I kind of liked it that way. Mrs. Callaghan's brother who came to mow the lawns said we should pull it out, and looked at me as if I was the one who should do it. He was a piano tuner, or at least that's what Mrs. Callaghan told me he did. She said he had a good ear.

I ran my hand over my shaved scalp. The skin was tingling, and hot, and sticky where I had nicked myself. Man, I was tired.

On the other side of the duplex the door opened and Dutch ambled out. Mrs. Callaghan put him out every morning at about the same time: you could set your watch by it. I sat still and he passed me like I wasn't there.

The tags on his collar jingled as he checked every bush and shrub along the perimeter. He wagged his tail when he came to the garden hose. He picked up the nozzle in his old jaws and chewed it a bit before he dropped it again. Then he glanced over his shoulder towards the light. Mrs. Callaghan whispered something. He went back to his work.

I would hear her talking to him all night through the wall. She would say something and he would answer with silence, the wrinkles forming on his big square head. They were a team. Mrs. Callaghan would walk Dutch to the corner store and he would walk her back. Their world was the one-bedroom apartment and the garden out back. They didn't worry about anything much that happened beyond it.

Mrs. Callaghan's shadow narrowed as it fell across the grass but it didn't move. She would just stand there and watch her old boy. She liked to sip tea from a matching cup and saucer. She hardly slept at all.

My mother was sleepless towards the end. She would sit by the window until all hours, looking out. The nurse didn't like it but I didn't think it was a problem. The city at night is wasted on sleep. I understood someone wanting to stay close to it. She'd go out for long walks or drive places and talk to people. She'd buy things she didn't even like. She was collecting as much of the outside world as she could before it moved out of reach, before the illness reduced her.

Her decline sharpened rapidly. In the last weeks it was all she could do to walk to the bathroom. When she became sensitive to light the blinds had to be drawn. Visitors told her stories about what was happening in the garden: if it was raining or the birds were singing or the time of day. A long time before she died, she was reduced to relying entirely on her memory: who she used to be; the things she'd done and said. The short distance beyond the window.

Dutch paused in the corner of the lawn. He had found his favourite spot. He sniffed the dirt. He started to dig.

I watched him for a while and then got up and found a business card for someone else I could pretend to be.

14.

I took a pair of paper overalls with me, changing into them behind a tree in the reserve. The overalls rasped as I crossed the playing fields. Joggers were working their way around the perimeter, gulping the cold air. The sky was halfway between last night and the day, marked with the barest blue.

At the end of the street the lights had been burning inside the Atlantic Pool & Gym since 5 a.m. Lines of people stood unmoving in the windows as they rowed and pedalled and ran, their heat and steam fogging the glass. The air outside was forgiving but inside the Atlantic it still looked like winter.

The ground floor car park was full. I went along the rows until I found the blue Mazda. It was an import. The Japanese safety stickers were still in the windows and the cassette buttons were labelled in red and white kanji. A pair of wraparound shades were lying in the hand brake tray.

Sometimes I got there early enough to see her take the shades off before she got out of the car. Other times I waited until she came out and drove away. She had a cool walk. She would throw her things in the back seat and lean against the door until she finished talking on the phone. She had an anti-theft brace locked across the steering wheel and a number 77 ten-inch wrench lying in the space between the driver's seat and the door. The wrench was for effect, not repairs: something to have handy for the long drive home.

There was a two-battery torch in the back seat underneath a crumpled map of the North Island. She liked to go snorkelling around Goat Island and take long walks at Kare Kare, but mostly she liked to swim.

* * *

I walked into the front entrance of the building as a red-faced kid was walking out, his wet hair spotting his collar. He spun the revolving door so hard it almost hit me. The guy behind the admissions desk saw it happen but didn't blink. He had clipped hair and a muscled neck and a face that said, fuck it: spin the door back. The name on his staff pin was Rosetti.

"Hey, Rosie." I put out my hand. He didn't like touching it. "I'm here to look at the filters," I said.

"They did that already," he said.

"I'm here to check the work for QA. You're familiar with our quality assurance programme?"

"No, I'm not."

"Quality assurance is the key to workplace safety and productivity. We initiated the process as part of an ongoing consultation with our clients. The goals are fairly straightforward—it's more process than outcome oriented—but the results have been pretty outstanding. Have you considered implementing a QA scheme for this business?"

"No idea, mate," he said, glancing at whoever was waiting in line behind me.

"We advocate customer focus—similar milestones to the type of services—"

"Look, just give me a number or something."

"No worries." I flicked him the business card. "Maybe you'd be interested in one of our presentations."

"Thanks," he said. I started telling him about the options but he was already looking past me. Someone else was coming through the door: he wanted to see how that would turn out.

* * *

Poolside sounded like a fight. The warm air stank of chlorine and sweat. The swimmers were pounding down the lanes so close they were hand to toe, churning the water white. Breakfast radio was playing over the indoor speakers, bouncing music off the low ceiling. Up top in the gym people on machines were slamming weights up and down. Exercycles whistled in unison as their riders pedalled towards the TV sets hanging from the ceiling. Everyone was rushing to get fit before they left for work.

Exhausted bathers were slumped in the spa. There was a queue for the sauna. A man in jandals and coloured shorts was shouting on his cell phone as he stood under the diving board, one dripping finger in his free ear. The terraced spectator seats were empty except for a well-dressed woman who was reading a newspaper. She had spread out her yellow raincoat so she wouldn't get wet. I lifted up the little grate at the end of the aisle and made out as though I was checking the drain.

Varina Sumich was swimming in the triathlon lane. She faced away from the terraces to breathe. She was wearing the second of her speed suits, the black one with the white loop around the shoulders. She wore two bathing caps: a red one on the back of her hair and the white one over that. She wasn't wearing flippers today but she was holding her own. Her stroke was as straight as a clock hand.

Varina loved the relentlessness of the water. She once described it as being cold until your body turned it warm; light but heavy. Beginners pushed it aside only to have it fall back to be pushed aside again. The trick, she said, was to slide right through.

I watched her finish the length. She pushed up her goggles and hung off the edge, wiping her eyes. Then she rolled to one side and began dipping under the lane floats towards the ladder on the other side.

She paused again at the railing. She'd been in the water for thirty minutes: her shoulders were burning. She stared into the middle distance as if contemplating this last effort and then hauled herself out.

Water streamed from her black suit as she walked over to

the bench. Her stride was unsteady. She always said a good swim turned your legs to jelly. She grabbed the zipper tape behind her neck and loosened the top of the suit. Her skin was pink underneath. Her pulse was jumping in her neck.

She unrolled the towel lying on the bench and shook her charm bracelet out of it. She had been collecting for the bracelet since she was thirteen. The trinkets were crowded and bunched up and the links were discoloured where they had been repaired. She always left it poolside when she went swimming. Varina liked to keep things close.

She dabbed her face with the towel. She ran the towel around her neck. She turned her head and looked up towards where I was sitting.

She waved.

The woman sitting in front of me waved back. She folded the newspaper and slipped it into an expensive-looking shoulder bag. She picked up the yellow raincoat she had been sitting on to keep dry and stepped down the steps to where Varina stood, her flat heels clicking on the wet cement.

I watched them shake hands. The woman was small-framed, maybe in her fifties, with a delicate neck and a straight jaw. Her fair hair was streaked with grey. She had an ankh around her neck but no other jewellery. Although Varina had waved first, the other woman was being more formal about it. Varina continued drying herself. She had a way of raising her chin when she was being told something she didn't want to hear. If the other woman was sensitive to the gesture she didn't show it. She went to take something from her bag but Varina shook her head, waving her towards the exit. The raincoat woman made a deferential gesture and walked away. Whoever she was, she had been waiting a long time to have a very short conversation. She was still waiting in the lobby when I walked out. The raincoat was folded over her briefcase and her hands were in her lap. She glanced up and I looked away.

The street was brighter but dirty. The morning traffic was picking up. The fast food restaurant opposite the Atlantic was shaped like a chateaux. I went inside and gulped down a Coke with extra ice, biting the cubes until they squeaked, waiting to see who came out.

Varina was still washing herself in the changing rooms. She would take off her speed suit in the shower and walk on it in the basin so the sweat washed out from the inside. Her towels she hung out on the line behind the apartment but the suits she kept in the stairwell. In summer they would dry overnight. In winter, it took longer. Tomorrow she would get up before dawn and put the second suit in her car and drive to the pool and start her lengths again.

15.

After Caroline had been gone for a certain amount of time the school put on parent and child evenings at the church hall. There was a tea urn waiting on a trestle table in the foyer for afterwards, when everyone had finished talking. The room smelled of dried flowers and milk.

The session was chaired by a woman named Susan. Susan had grey hair and a straight nose and a soft, deep voice. She wore a long waistcoat over her sweater and a green bead neck-lace and sandals and a turquoise ring. She stood at the centre of the chairs as she talked so she could facing each audience mem-ber in turn. She moved her hands as she spoke, resting one in the other as if it was getting tired.

"Thank you all so much for coming tonight," Susan said. "It's so great to see you. I'm really looking forward to sharing with you."

The kids were sitting around with their parents. A girl with her arm in plaster. A freckled boy with a red nose. Tracy McAlpine was squeezed between her mother and her father. The left lens of her horn-rimmed spectacles was tinted to encourage her lazy right eye. Varina Sumich was wearing a brown Adidas tracksuit top. Her father was sitting next to her, looking angry. He was short in the legs: sitting next to her, he looked just as tall. His fists were huge.

Susan clutched her hand for a second and then opened it again.

"It's a difficult time for everybody here. I'm sure you're experiencing a range of emotions right now. Maybe you want to be here. Maybe you don't. Maybe you're afraid—thinking, will this happen to me? What about my children?"

She turned to her left.

"I know we're all missing Caroline. We're worried because she's our friend. Losing a member of our community frightens us because we're all connected, each and every one of us: if someone leaves, it means we lose part of ourselves. Even if we don't acknowledge that, we feel it, deep within us and that's why it's hard to talk about. We feel she's gone and we're worried about it. We're upset."

She turned.

"The way it goes is this," she said. "We're here to talk, to share. Anyone who wants to ask for time, just raise your hand, and you can have as long as you'd like to speak. When you've finished, I'll ask other people to contribute. We don't want there to be any pressure so if you're a little shy or can't find the right words, I might ask you to share, and maybe ask you some questions. We're here to talk about ourselves and to discover the truth. Yeah? How is that?"

Her smile widened.

"Are there any questions?"

Tracy put up her hand.

"Hi," Susan said. "What's your name?"

"Um, Tracy."

"Hi Tracy. Would you mind standing up so we can all hear you?"

"Um, okay." Tracy's chair squeaked as she pushed it back.

"Are you a friend of Caroline's, Tracy?"

Tracy hesitated. "I knew her from school."

"And do you have a question?"

"I was wondering, um, where your necklace came from."

"It's from Mexico."

"Is that like in South America?"

"That's right, yes. It's near there."

"Thank you."

"What do you think about Caroline?" Susan said. "Are you scared because she's disappeared?"

"I just wonder where she is."

"How does that make you feel, Tracy?"

"I don't know."

"How do you feel about Caroline?"

"I don't know."

Tracy sat down. Her mother touched her arm. Tracy straightened her tinted spectacles. Varina tilted her chin back, counting the rafters.

"What do other people think about what Tracy has shared with us?" Susan said. "How do other people feel?"

Nobody answered.

I felt myself crouch, waiting for it to blow over like everything else. Susan was looking around into people's eyes, trying to catch them. I was thinking about how I should look away when I realised that she was staring straight at me and I was staring back, and it was my turn, and there was nothing I could do. I swallowed.

"My name is Mark," I said, and stood up.

I said I was scared to sleep. I thought I was making it up at first but by the time I'd finished I realised that I wasn't, and that it showed in my face, and that Susan was pleased to see the confusion reveal itself.

"Thank you very much for sharing that with us, Mark," she said. "Would anyone else like to contribute to what Mark has said?"

One of the other boys put up his hand to say that he couldn't sleep either. The girls started to talk about their nightmares. They described dreams about Caroline being happy or sad or asleep or angry. They had met her on the beach in the sun. They were sitting next to her in class or on the bus but then they woke up, and she was gone.

* * *

I lay awake that night listening to our old house talk. The villa's finial was broken at the stump. The roof over the porch had rusted in concentric circles. The spring rain twisted from the lacy holes and broke into spray, pattering on the black wood verandah. The front steps had rotted to the point of collapse.

At midnight I got up and put on my black Aerosmith T-shirt and black jeans and black basketball boots and climbed out the window. I walked up the road in the moonlight.

The letter box of Tracy McAlpine's house was shaped like a dovecot. The window panes were bright blue. The front lawn was soft with no prickles. The garage was empty. The spare key was on a nail beside the window.

I unlocked the back door of the house and walked inside.

The kitchen was empty. There were oranges in the fruit bowl. I drank some milk. I rinsed the glass and stood it on the bench.

The blue fell in strips between the banisters. There was a double bed in the parents' room. Under the mattress on Mr. McAlpine's side was a brochure with a green cover. The pages inside were all colour photographs of women outdoors in plaits and knee socks.

Tracy's name was on a ceramic plaque on her bedroom door. The bookcase was lined with her old toys: dolls, puzzles, pretend jewellery, a fake leather diary with a tinny clasp. The clothes in the drawers were folded and soft. The wardrobe smelled of perfume.

She had a white blouse that was sort of like Caroline's. I took it off the hanger and laid it on the bed. I arranged a pair of her flared jeans below the blouse and then some of the other things, trying to work out how they went together.

I saw Tracy out walking a few days later. I was riding towards her. She was with one of her friends. Her arms were folded and she was looking down. I rang the bell but she still didn't look up. I had to ride up on the grass to avoid hitting her. I had an urge to say I was sorry and at the same time to deny that it had been me but I couldn't decide and by then it was too late and she had gone. The bike's front wheel left a skid of brown mud through the grass. There were flowers growing along the side of the footpath: daisies, or something like that.

16.

Harry Bishop held a press conference. He told the reporters that the break-in at the McAlpine residence was not related to the missing girl. The newspapers ran the stories anyway. Caroline had been stalked by a killer. Caroline had been kidnapped and taken away. A conspiracy was at work to abduct our children: a sect, a cabal.

House owners in each street met to roster patrols. Parents carpooled to transport the children after school. Teachers at the crossing asked eight-year-olds to identify the adults collecting them. The kids squinted at their parents in the sunlight, wondering.

Play was monitored in parks. People bought dogs, put up signs. Teenagers started to make shivs, filing down kitchen knives in the garage. Residents built fences out of rough pine. They hung mesh curtains and left the guest light burning. They slept with wrenches and cricket bats beside the bed.

Harry Bishop appeared on television with his face scrunched up. He made a personal promise that there would be no more break-ins around the head. Nobody believed him.

* * *

The line of *Missing Girl* posters outside the Masonic Tavern had softened in the rain. Caroline's smile had become wrinkled under the streetlights.

I got an old boatie with grey hair and split tennis shoes to get me some beers. I gave him money for half a dozen and he came back with four, which was fair enough. He glanced at the posters as I screwed the bottles into my coat pockets. It's no good about that girl, he said: you shouldn't be out yourself.

I walked over to the beach.

The tide had dragged the moon up on the sand. The red and green lights of the boats were crossing the channel, far out in the darkness. I spread out my coat and sat down and opened a beer with my pocket knife and drank. It tasted alright.

I looked at the water for a long time before I noticed any movement. There was a swimmer moving across the bay, splashing. It wasn't unusual to see people swimming at night. People swam around North Head all year round. The water was warm in the shallows. But to swim then, during the news reports and the police patrols—that was something.

The splashes tracked in a slow arc. The swimmer was coming closer. The pattern broke and turned towards shore. I crouched to hide my moon shadow.

Varina Sumich stood and walked out of the sea, her stride splashing the breakers. She pulled her plastic goggles down around her neck. She walked up the sand and picked up her towel, panting. She blew a line of snot out of her nose. She pulled on her sweatpants, the stretch fabric sticking to her wet skin. She zipped her top up under her chin and pulled off her rubber cap. She tipped her head to one side and towelled her wet hair as she left the beach, her bare feet tracking the sand.

* * *

The Sumichs left the house on Thursdays. They had cement animals in their front yard. The flamingo was stiff. The tiger was asleep. The garage smelled of oil and dirt. The tools on the wall were outlined in white. It was all very organised, and there was no key on the shelves.

I walked around the house a couple of times before I noticed that the bedroom window was open just a crack. The latch handle was up. I stood on tip-toe and took the ledge in both hands and hung there for a moment, listening. There was no movement. I climbed inside.

My shoes squeaked on the wooden floor. The room smelled of woollen blankets and paper. There was a single bed in the corner and a dresser with a mirror and a writing desk. Flowery decals and pictures were pinned on the walls: pop groups, actresses, family photographs, homework, poems, drawings of flowers. A square of moonlight picked out a picture on the wall: Caroline.

The photo showed Varina and Caroline together. They were standing in the driveway in their swimming costumes. Both girls had their arms around each other. Varina stood taller than

Caroline. She was in the same costume she had been wearing the other night. Caroline's suit was patterned and she had a towel wrapped around her waist. I reached out and put my hand across Varina and Caroline was left alone laughing at whoever was taking the picture, smiling in front of the pine needles. It was the photograph from the poster. *Missing Girl.* I stared.

There was a click.

It sounded like a lock. I stood there listening.

The door shut. There was a shout.

Mr. Sumich was walking up the hallway to his daughter's room. I turned and froze.

Varina was sitting up in the sheets, watching me. She pointed at the floor below the bed.

"Quick," she said. "He's coming."

I rolled under the bed as her father switched on the lights. I could see his shoes walk towards me as he crossed the floor. Her father had seen that her window was open. She said it was too hot to sleep with it closed. But he saw someone as he was coming up the driveway. He must have imagined it. She wanted to go to sleep now.

She must never have the window open, ever. Not in the house by herself. It was time for him to go to bed. She had to promise him not to do that again. She promised.

The mattress sank as Varina rolled over. Her father's feet turned and walked away. The room went dark. The door clicked shut. I stared at the mattress scrim.

Varina reached over the side of the bedstead and wiggled her fingers.

"He's drunk," she whispered. "He'll go to sleep straight away."

We listened to her father as he crashed around the house, slamming doors. He dropped something in the bathroom. He flushed the toilet. He ran the sink tap full and screwed it shut until the pipes creaked. He was talking to himself, angrily; talking to her, if she'd been listening. And then something else went thud and the last crack of light disappeared.

I listened to my breath. The dust from the sacking fell into my eyes.

"He's asleep," Varina said.

I crawled out from under the bed. Varina slid to the edge of the mattress.

"He's been at the Masonic," she said. "He always comes back and shouts."

"I was at the Masonic last week."

"Did you see him?"

"Not to go inside. I got a man to buy me some beer. The old guy who walks around."

"I know him."

"Yeah."

She had her chin in her hands. Her eyes were dark.

"Detective Bishop drinks," she said. "I could smell it on his breath at school."

"He keeps a bottle in the glove box of his car."

"He came round here to talk to my father," Varina said. "He was asking questions about Tracy."

"He came round to my place, too. He was really pissed off."

"What about?"

"I don't know. My mother asked him to leave."

"I was scared," Varina said.

"I wasn't," I said.

"He wants to know about the McAlpines. About the break-in."

"I don't care."

"You don't want to get caught," she said.

"He can't catch anyone," I said. "He doesn't know where Caroline's gone. They don't know anything."

Varina wiped her nose.

"I don't know where she is," she said.

"I don't know, either."

She looked at the photograph on the wall.

"He took that photo. They said they wanted a photo of Caroline. He didn't tell me they were going to use it for the poster."

"Did they pay you for it?"

"It was for the search."

"He carries a gun. You can see it under his jacket."

She nodded. "I saw his wife on the TV," she said. "She was interviewed after the search. The journalists asked how she would feel if it was her daughter who disappeared. She said they didn't have any children. Sometimes you can't have children, if you're an alcoholic."

"He was burned in a fire," I said. "His legs are all burned. It's why he wears long pants all the time."

She pulled the blanket around her shoulders.

"I saw you outside," she said.

"I like walking at night. I can't sleep."

"I remember you said that, at the counselling."

"It's so dumb, that thing."

"How's that woman who does it?" Varina winced. "She's so uncool."

"They're all uncool," I said. "They'll never find out what happened."

* * *

We talked until morning. We never raised our voices above a whisper. And then as the sky began to lighten I said I'd better go and she nodded and I slid out from under the bed. I said thanks and she said that's okay. When her father sobered up he would report the prowler but at that hour he was still drunk and snoring, and the only sound in the streets was the birds. I looked at her resting on her elbow in the bed, sizing her up. She had been one step ahead all along.

I left the same way I came in.

17.

Flight 901 was due to return on the same day it left: Wednesday, 28 November 1979. The bland announcement that it was late had to be decoded by someone who was older than us. What it meant was that the plane had crashed.

There were uninformed hopes that the plane had gone down in the ocean around the Antarctic Circle. We thought of life rafts bobbing in the water like the drawings in a safety manual. We talked about helicopters and people swimming away. We knew that snow was white and the tip of the world was small and that anyone on it would be easy to find.

The impact was confirmed twelve hours later when a Navy plane spotted wreckage on the slope of Mount Erebus. Wind and cloud prevented a closer look. The photograph published in the next day's newspapers looked like a scorch mark in the middle of blank paper. The lack of detail felt like a cheat. The indistinct smear could have been anything. It didn't look like death: it hinted at it. It was the first glimpse of the worst fear, like a dusted thumb print, or a lesion on an X-ray.

* * *

Over the next few days, TV crews and newspaper reporters travelled to Antarctica with the search teams. They were handed earplugs and lunch in a brown paper bag before climbing on board the military Star Lifter. The searchers were anonymous and identical in their round boots and salopettes and big, hooded jackets. They wore sunglasses and sweat bands and the same clench on their faces. The broadest men looked thin in the cold, the wind flapping their scarves like banners. They put up in new towns of pyramid tends and worked roped grids of flapping flags. The pennants were coloured but we were shown only black and white: black shards and black smears and black metal. Grey snow.

The reporters and police photographers chronicled the recovery operation as it spread out against the featureless slope. At first the blurred parts of the wreckage were easier to take in than the larger components of the plane. The parts that were recognisable were hard to believe: rows of seats; an intact door; the tail fin jutting out like an advertising billboard.

The plane had hit the mountain belly first so the fuselage buckled around the exploding wing. The lower engines had broken off and rolled flaming in the snow, bursting their smooth outer skin. Analysts felt the exposed bundles of piping and wire with gloved hands. The air was dry and the sun in the reflected metal was hot. They sweated as they worked. Perspiration froze along the jawline.

From time to time a curtain of low cloud would draw across the side of the mountain and close everything in, but generally they sweated in dirty grey snow and the black wreckage under a clear sky. It was summer in Antarctica and the weather was good.

Birds circled, drawn by the smell. Some bodies were in the open. Some had fallen into crevasses in the ice. Some were in pieces. The searchers buried the bodies in the snow to protect them from the big brown gulls. They wrapped them in black rubber bags. They fired shots in the air. They were appalled at first but then they became too tired to be appalled, and finally they just lapsed into working. It was a whole different world, a bad place at a worse time. 237 listed passengers and 20 flight staff and crew had died and it was gory work and no good would come of it. It was horrible: worse than anything anyone could have imagined. The sheer spectacle of it, the silent proof of the explosions and fire, overtook them. There was no guilt in it. Nobody knew how they should behave.

The rescue teams worked different sections of the scene. They marked each pile with numbers and put the numbers on a list. They didn't talk much. They pegged out flags and pyra-mid tents and wooden poles and tape fluttering in the cold wind. White snow. Black window. Black metal. Something else.

The odour was masked by the aviation fuel but it came up every once in a while. In a wind the slope smelled like toilet cleaner and kerosene. It burned the back of their throats. They broke off to retch and resumed work without comment. The nausea would pass. The nausea would come back.

They learned this along with the other rules of the ice. They were told to watch each other for signs of hypothermia: slurred speech, loss of balance, fatigue. Frostnip turns the skin red, then pale, then waxy white. Don't get exhausted. Cover your lips and nose. The faster the air moves, the more heat it drags away. Never remove your gloves.

They built new towns of pyramid tents and sat inside talking about anything except what they were doing. They listened to broadcasts on the shortwave. They smoked and ate. They slept, but they didn't really sleep. And in the morning they rolled out of their sleeping bags and began sorting between the flags and the bodies for anything that would identify who was there. Nights were as bright as day, but they were working in the dark.

The searchers and police teams didn't know who they were looking for. The sight seeing flight was a round trip that was listed as a domestic route. The classification required boarding passengers to hold nothing more than a ticket. There were no passports. The name on the booking didn't have to be theirs.

The passengers on the flight carried only hand luggage. Many didn't even have wallets. During the flight, they changed their seats, moved around the cabin to talk to other people or check the view from different windows. A lot of them had been block-booked in groups by travel agents, with no names on the tickets at all. Some of the passengers had turned up in place of a friend or relative.

Sometimes it turned out that the person in question had never got on board. Sometimes they were with the wrong person: a secretary; another woman's husband. Some people had taken the flight without telling anyone. An air hostess agreed to fill in for her best friend. A family won their tickets as a prize. A man who was scared of flying didn't want to get on board. His friends talked him into it.

Police rang around to confirm who had intended to take the flight. They typed up reports. They came up with a possible list of names that the searchers could match against what they had found, and gradually the identification became a process of elimination.

The searchers looked for photographs, documents, clothing, shoes, jewellery. They combed the snow for cuff links, tie pins, belt buckles, earrings, spectacles. Frozen cloth broke as it was peeled. Charred paper fluttered away. They found an outline in the ice. They opened a woman's purse. They recorded the length and colour of hair.

The news came through in whispers, at first: that they had found a new outline in the ice: a teenage girl stretched out in the snow. She had no name at first. It was in the paper, or someone heard it off the radio or maybe it was secret, because they didn't want you to know, and then they gave her a name. Caroline May.

* * *

The nature of the flight meant that some of the passengers could not be identified. They could have been anyone.

Anyone. And so in our minds we went digging and found her lying there in the ice and snow.

A long time had passed since Caroline walked out. Nobody knew what had happened. There was no indication that she might turn up at the time or place she eventually did. Even the rumours had not come close. Caroline had been found thousands of miles away. Her life became hourglass-shaped, the unknown marked by its narrow neck. Everything else could be seen except the point of transition.

The police had search photographs and facts and eyewitness accounts but nothing that would fill the space. Now we had answers. She had been travelling with an older man or a group of people or a couple or another woman. She'd had a child. She'd been married. She had stowed away in the cargo hold. She'd been drugged.

There were more questions, then, whispered by everyone who knew her. Caroline rolled over on the couch, turning her back to them all.

* * *

Harry Bishop stood outside the fire station as the search headquarters was dismantled. He watched his officers carrying out the tables and filing cabinets. He watched them load the chart of Caroline into the van. His staff were reassigned or sent on leave. The equipment was distributed around other offices. The case files were archived at the central station. The police were given leaves before being reassigned. The file boxes were loaded into cars and driven away.

Our classroom at school was rearranged. Caroline's desk was removed. One of the reporters came back. Someone tried to photograph the desk. Something in ballpoint was scratched in the lid.

The first days of summer arrived numb and still. Blooms of bare dirt broke out across the playing fields, waiting for the rain.

* * *

The last swim of the year was an organised ritual. The boys were bombing off the side to impress the girls, knees hugged to their chest. Kids were scattered around inside the fence, stretched in the sun. They pressed themselves wet on the cement and watched their silhouettes dry out. The air smelled of chlorine and wet grass. The insects were stuck on the same note, over and over.

Varina Sumich walked out on the diving board. Her toes curled over the end. Water dripped from her hands. I watched her, shivering, waiting for her to dive, but she had stopped. She was looking at something on the other side of the fence.

Harry Bishop was staggering across the playing fields, his black police shoes kicking up dirt. His loosened tie was flapping around his neck and his face was red and he was clutching a nearly empty vodka bottle, the last measure of alcohol swilling as he walked.

The kids laughed and started crowding the fence to watch the drunk stumbling towards them. Harry was talking to himself, stomping across the dried earth like it was a tilting deck. When he reached the fence he put out his arm and leaned on it, his weight bending the mesh. The boys whispered. The girls giggled. Harry fumbled for the bottle's cap before realising it was already unscrewed. He chugged back the vodka and coughed, wiping his lips with the back of his hand.

Varina stared at Harry. Harry stared at her. The spit ran down his wrist in strings. She looked down at the water below the tip of the board and then looked back at him. Harry wouldn't break his stare. Varina had been right when she said he was a drinker, and he was looking at her like he knew what she had said. He spilled the last of the bottle as he finished it. The run off blackened his tie.

The first sign that this was really happening was when the teacher opened the gate and stepped outside. She hadn't worked out who Harry was but as she came closer she must have recognised him from the sick room. Harry ignored her. He kept staring at Varina as she stood on the diving board, shivering in the sun. The teacher paused, giving Harry one last chance to spare them both the embarrassment. And then suddenly Varina dived, making a perfect arc before she disappeared.

Harry saw the splash and shook his head. He grinned at the teacher. He dropped the empty bottle. It bounced. He did the best he could to stand straight as he started back across the yellow ground.

18.

The Grey Lynn Festival brings out the doctors and TV producers and business professionals who have moved into the suburb over the last decade, but the stalls are still run by the Islanders and hippies who were there before that when the steep streets and worker's cottages were cheap and less than fashionable. You don't need a licence to sell: all you do is turn up in the morning and pay the organisers and set out your collection of velvet paintings or secondhand clothes or old paperback novels everyone has read. You can sell shellfish knocked off the rocks at a beach where harvesting is prohibited or undersize crayfish or seedlings grown from cuttings taken from a native reserve. You can sell whitebait out of season or designer T-shirts printed in a Hong Kong sweat shop or cheap sunglasses that don't protect your eyes and music CDs burned on a home PC.

The streets were busy with crowds of people travelling to and from the park. The fathers were well-upholstered in dark green or navy or white T-shirts, with walk shorts and boat shoes. The mothers wore long sleeveless dresses and expensive summer

sandals. Their children had sunglasses and coloured zinc oint-
ment on their faces. Babies were slung in tricycle prams with
giant wheels designed to be pushed by new parents while they
jogged to keep in shape. Everybody was smiling. I lit a cigarette.

I joined a queue for organic coffee. A family had set up a
stand in the overgrown front yard of their creaky weatherboard
villa. The coffee was being made on an Italian machine on a trestle table with wires and piping running past the old station
wagon parked in the driveway. Mum had red hair and a rat's tail
plaited down to her waist and a No Nukes T-shirt and dad had
a goatee and silver wraparounds and a studded lip. Their friends
were sitting around on a sofa dragged out onto the yellowing
grass while their children counted out the customers' change.
The girl had soft limbs and the boy had curly hair and they both
had the perfect, buttery brown tan kids get from playing outside
all their lives.

The mother filled the paper cup to the brim. It was hot
enough to burn my hand. I quickly drank enough for the girl
to cool it down with iced soya milk from a ceramic jug. The
sugar was unrefined brown crystals in a paper bag on the oilskin tablecloth and the spoons were wet plastic. Brightly
coloured paper streamers were hanging underneath the *Coffee
For Sale* sign, fluttering in a cool breeze nobody could feel. It
was early morning in late November, and summer was starting
to come up.

I sipped the coffee as I walked. The north entrance to the
festival was roped off so the stall owners had somewhere to
park their cars. Sedans and four-wheel drives were maneuver-
ing one empty space at a time. I stayed on the walkway, bump-
ing along with the families and prams.

At the back of the car park where the rope ended campaign-
ers were distributing leaflets about education and genetic mod-
ification and electoral reform. People took the flyers and
dropped them a few steps later. The halo of discarded papers

marked the border where the bustle became a distraction from everything else.

Even behind their sunglasses, people were walking between the pyramid tents and stalls with a glazed expression. It might have been the heat or the hour, and some of the teenagers could have been drinking or swapping joints before they got dressed up and came down to the park, but mostly it was the obliging mask you see people wearing in a shopping center or busy traffic, a glaze of half-interest and deference like a shrug. They bumped shoulders as they pushed past but there was no need to say sorry. Ten o'clock and they looked like they had been there all their lives.

The performers' stage was set up on the south side of the park by the half-pipe. Kids sat around the PA system cradling their boards and spinning the wheels with their fingers while their fellow skaters took turns. They would hunker down and tip off the edge and then shoot up again a moment later on either side of the rim, a scramble of limbs and big shorts. I used to skate. I was pretty good at it until I got tall and my center of gravity shifted. I guess I could have stuck with it but I didn't. The idea of starting over was too frustrating.

The tents had been arranged in islands between the lanes of people. They were all around the same size, about six feet square, and their bright nylon walls were rolled up and tied so you could see through each block like an X-ray, all the different things for sale laid out. The vendors had attached crystals to the flaps and wind chimes and more coloured streamers that cast ragged patches of shade.

The wet odour of barbecue was blowing from the east side of the park where the food carts were lined up. Hot dog sticks and tomato sauce packets were trampled into the grass. The cooking was being done under a big line of nylon and canvas awnings on gas stoves that ran off camping cylinders. Each stand had its own lantern burning in the daylight. The prices and menus were on leaning blackboards and hand painted signs. There was Chinese and Thai and Japanese; vegetarian, fish and chips, Indian. There was soup cooking, and fish, and seared meat sliced into dark, sugary sauce. You could buy fried peppers and chicken on stick, mushrooms wrapped in something pale, thin noodles. People were sitting to eat in the shade of the bamboo bushes on the bank, hunched so they didn't drop grease on their clothes. Flies were hanging in the air. The seagulls were looking for scraps around the food bins.

A guy in a red bandanna was sweating over the grilling plate in his kebab stall. The satay sticks were stacked as high as his shoulder. The meat was the same bright yellow both cooked or raw. He laid them out in a lidded polystyrene tray with his bare hands and dressed them with watery sauce. I ate as I walked. The food and drink was good, considering. When I was finished and nobody was looking I took the bundle of jewellery out of my pocket, put it inside the white plastic tray and closed the lid.

* * *

Lennox's stall was on the corner of an intersection—a good spot. He was sitting in a director's chair in the green shade of the tent flap, surrounded by shapes and carvings in dark wood. He was wearing a pale straw hat and an Hawaiian shirt and the same kind of geeky walk shorts the working fathers had on. He leaned back in the canvas chair with his skinny legs crossed and his chin resting thoughtfully in his finger and thumb as a big, cheerful woman on the other side of the table inspected a carving of a dolphin. She was chatting to Lennox as she turned it in her hands and he was nodding and smiling pleasantly, letting her hold it until it became familiar.

"It's so heavy," she said.

"It's solid," Lennox said.

"It's teak, isn't it?"

"I think it's pulaulu wood, that one."

"The work that's gone into it . . ."

"Hand finished."

"It's a god, the dolphin. It's a Buddhist symbol. With the calf, see? It's a symbol of motherhood."

Lennox nodded, listening. "I can tell you know a bit about it," he said.

"We went to Bali years ago."

"It's a beautiful country."

"It's just gorgeous," she said. "Just gorgeous. The beautiful beaches. Where did you go?"

"My wife likes it down south."

"It's beautiful down there." She nodded, turning the carving over again. "Just beautiful."

"There's a discount on that."

"Is there?"

"Fifteen per cent," Lennox said. "People usually buy them in pairs, you see, but we only brought in the one."

"So this is the only one?" she said. "It's unique?"

"Yeah." He scratched behind his ear as if that was just another detail and he didn't care about it either way.

She bought it. Lennox counted out her change and pretended to be interested in a story about her Bali trip for a few more minutes. He slipped the dolphin carving into a paper bag and tried to interest her in a polishing oil that would replenish the teak as sun and visitors and the Auckland weather threatened the finish over time but the woman already had some stuff at home, a little bottle of the red oil from the supermarket, Ekko or something—did he know it? Lennox said he didn't, and the woman thanked him and walked off with the carving that had always been hers.

When she had gone Lennox glanced over like I was just another customer.

"Love the hair," he said.

"Have you ever actually been to Bali?"

"I saw a doco about it on the Discovery Channel once. Looks like a lovely place. Tui's been there heaps. She used to go with her first husband when he was grading steel or something—I dunno. She was the one who put me onto the market for this stuff. Why don't you come and take the weight off?"

"Cheers."

I stepped around the ropes. It was cool underneath the canvas. The shaded breeze seemed stronger. The lawn was streaked with yellow under the bench tables. Lennox nodded at a second director's chair behind him. I pulled it up and sat down.

"So how's business?"

"Bloody good. I've sold one of these already." He tapped a snarling mask that was hanging next to him, its striped eyeballs bulging red and gold and white. "Imagine hanging that in your flat. Eh? Jesus. And check this out."

He lifted a bridge no bigger than his hand with peasants crossing its cracked planking, some of them frozen with loads on their backs, others with fishing poles. There was even a man on a bicycle with tiny spoked wheels.

"Look at the work in that," he said. "That's taken somebody fucking hours."

"Is that ivory?"

"It's water buffalo horn."

"They cut off their horns?"

He nodded. "Trim them once a year. That's what it says in the brochure. Every piece comes with a printed tag and a gift box. You lose that pretty smartly, of course."

"A brochure's not too native craftsman, is it?"

"They're fucking craftsmen, alright. They turn these out in factory quantities at ten dollars a piece." He nodded to the tray in my hand. "You want me to get rid of that for you?"

"Thanks."

"Pop it in the bin." He kicked over a cardboard box filled with crushed wrappers and string. "I'll take that home later. All the stall owners have to sign a contract saying they'll keep the place tidy."

"That's very conscientious of you."

I dropped the satay tray into the box. The weight of the jewellery made a soft thud. Lennox made a happy face as he slid the box back beside his chair.

"That feels like a night's work," he said.

"Good."

"Listen, mate," he said. "It might be a while longer before I can get that money to you."

"That's no problem."

"Are you sure?"

"I'm sure."

"I hate putting you out like that. I just get the feeling that the guy might not come through like he said."

"What can you do."

"Have you got enough to get by?"

"I'll be fine."

"Feel free to take a couple of pieces for your girlfriend or something."

"I'd never do that," I said. "She's got plenty of stuff."

Lennox grinned. "Sounds like it went all right."

"Just like you said."

"Bump into anyone?"

"Nearly."

"I saw something about it."

"I don't really read the papers."

"Aw, they never say much. They're full of rubbish, nowadays." He scratched his nose. "So are you going to take some time off, now?"

"I might."

"Remember what we talked about. You're up against the law of averages in a small town. More people notice who comes and goes than you think."

"I never tell anyone what I do. I never bring anyone home."

"What about your girlfriend?"

"Never. You're the only person who visits, Len."

"I'm flattered."

I looked out at the crowd.

"You've never told anyone where I live," I said, phrasing it as if it wasn't a question.

Lennox squinted beneath the brim of his neat little hat.

"Did something happen?" he said.

"Someone left me a note."

"Jesus." He sucked air through his teeth. "What did it say?"

"It didn't say anything."

"Was it a joke? An old friend?"

"I'm not sure."

"Where was it—in the letter box?"

I didn't say anything.

"Tell me it wasn't inside the house."

I looked at him.

"Fuck," Lennox said. "Where are you going to go?"

I shrugged.

"You're not going to hang around, right?"

I said nothing. Lennox shook his head. He unwrapped a bundle of newspapers to reveal an identical carving of a dolphin and its calf. He blew the sawdust off it and stood it where the first had been.

19.

Mr. Stillaman's BMW was brand new. Josie took my skull in both hands as I climbed inside.

"It's like a whole different you," she said, stroking my scalp. "You've got a good head. Some people have a head that's the wrong shape but you don't—you have a good head."

"I'm pleased."

"Me, too. It brings me closer to your thoughts."

She drove us out in Titirangi. The corners of the road were blind. The white lines along the shoulder were hidden by the hanging ferns and trees. The Fire Risk billboard predicted safe conditions because vandals had torn off the arrow.

Josie's clients lived in a five-acre section of cloud forest. I waited in the car while she delivered the papers to the door. It was a nice place. The architecture was 1960s style with low overlapping sections. The laundry window was on the ground floor. I turned to look at it as we drove out.

"What is it?" Josie said.

"It's nothing."

"You sure?"

"Keep going."

"I don't have to take the car back," she said. "We could go walk on the beach."

A light rain was falling on the coast. The sea was milk and the sand was grey. We crossed the dunes with our heads under her raincoat. Her shorter stride fell in with mine, lining up every other step. The rain pattering on the oilskin sounded impatient, like fingers drumming on a desk.

"Do you want to go back and look at the house?" she said.

"Just for fun," I said.

"Sure," she said. "For fun."

* * *

A mist fell with the sunset and erased the details of the forest. The road turned grey before slipping into darkness with everything else. Now and then something moved through the scrub—a bird or a rat shaking the dead leaves on the ground. And then, soon, we couldn't even see the gaps in the trees.

Her clients left the house around nine. Their headlights twisted through the trees and disappeared. The bush fell dark again. Josie's shoulder was rigid. I slipped my hand under her seat belt. Her heart was beating fast.

"Nobody can see us," I promised. "Nobody knows we're here."

She bit her lip, staring at the fog.

"Maybe we should wait," she said

"You want to back out?"

She blinked. She wanted to say yes. She wanted to change her mind but she couldn't back out. Not now. She shook her head.

"It's natural to be scared on your first time," I said.

She pulled into the driveway with the brakes barely squeaking. Moths and crawling bugs had collected around the security light. I took a deep breath. The oxygen cleared my head for a moment and then my heart beat fast again. I could feel the blood in my face. I told myself that I was staying sharp.

"You stay here," I said.

"I want to come with you."

"Stay."

I took a walk around the property. A wire fence ran down to a gate. A wheelbarrow stood by the garden hose. There was a spade and plant food and gardening gloves. Food tins and plastic were piled in a recycling bin. Old newspapers were bundled for collection. The sidewalk was scrubbed clean. The lawn had been freshly cut.

Josie jumped when I knocked on her door. She got out and I held her hand as I led her down to the laundry window.

"I think I heard something," she said.

"There's nobody for miles."

"You can't make any noise. You can't make a mess."

"I won't."

She watched as I opened the newspapers and spread them across the window. I wet them down with the hose and the soaked maché stuck to the glass like clay. I smoothed out the pulp. I wiggled my fingers into the gardening gloves, breaking off the dried grass and mud. And then I punched the center of the window. Slowly the mulch of glass and pulp peeled away and slumped onto the floor.

Josie's smile was almost hidden in the moonlight, but not quite.

She caught her skirt climbing through the window. I could see the white triangle of torn cloth flapping in the moonlight. I put my arm tight around her waist and kissed her. And then I took her hand and led her upstairs to the lounge.

* * *

Our shadows walked along the hall. The lounge was wide and quiet. Josie stayed half a step behind me, drifting between the pieces of furniture. She surprised herself by yawning. You get tired, breaking in. The tension wears you down. On my first job, I practically fainted when I got inside. The minutes afterwards were a gap in time, like a dream.

I poured us drinks.

"Here's to DNA," she said.

"I don't think mine's on record."

She tapped my glass. "It is now. Standard procedure."

"That's only for murders and shit. Cheers."

"So am I the first girl you've broken in with?"

"I wouldn't call it breaking in."

"What would you call it?"

"I don't know."

"Like a holiday." She smiled. "I can tell I'm your first." She sank into the white leather couch and ran her hands along the cushions. "I'm totally sick of my apartment. Seeing this makes it worse." She giggled. "It is like a trip. Like another world. And I can't tell anybody."

"You can if you want."

"I can't. I don't want to. It'll be our secret."

She unfolded her legs, squelching the shiny upholstery. She spread her arms and tipped back her head. And then she sat up straight again, looking at me as if I were a stranger and I remembered that we were the only people in the room, and that she was close, and I could smell her.

"What shall we do?" she said.

"Just what you're doing."

She blinked in the blue light, the stars floating above the forest. She looked at me, stretching. She wiggled her glass. I poured us more.

"Thank you very much," she said.

"You're welcome."

Her smile was becoming drowsy. She was thinking to herself the way she did when she walked alone. Her eyelids were heavy. She crossed her legs and then looked up at me. Her stare was electric.

"May I smoke?"

"It's not my place."

"Would you like a cigarette?"

"Yes."

"Yes, thank you," she corrected.

"Yes, thank you."

She handed me the pack.

"What brand of cigarettes are these?" she said.

"Marlboros."

"I'm sorry, I don't understand."

"These are Marlboro cigarettes."

"I would like a Marlboro cigarette, please." She took one. "Do you have a light?"

I slipped the lighter out of my pocket without breaking our line of vision. The flame popped out of my hand. She cupped it in her fingers and leaned forward with the cigarette in between her lips. Her touch was delicate: steady. The flame caught the paper. She drew in smoke and sat back.

She opened her legs.

The alcohol mixed as I kissed her. I reached around her waist. She held the kiss, her breath hissing through her nostrils. Her cheeks were damp. Her face was hot. I got tangled on the buttons, kissing her smooth neck, her clavicle, the swell of her breast. She flicked her head back. I pressed down, pulling her underneath me. She broke away and swallowed, her face turning from side to side. I held it.

"I'm cold," she said.

"I want you to be cold."

I pulled up her dress.

"Mark," she said.

I pushed against her. She coughed. I pushed my fingers inside her briefs. She was soft. Her hands held my face. I was grinding against her now. Her eyes were looking somewhere else. She wasn't looking.

I made her wait until I went outside. I stood on the back lawn and she stood against the window. She started slowly undoing the buttons of her top. She lay down on the sofa. She rolled over on it, the curve of her buttocks against the leather, the curving line dark in the room. I took the edge of the balcony and lifted myself up. I put my hand on the pane, moved my shadow across her shoulder.

The sliding doors wobbled and she turned, startled. She hadn't heard me approach. She had no idea I was so close. Her mouth made a shape. She clapped her arms across her chest. She was glaring at me, blonde in the blue, and her eyes were suddenly black.

* * *

We said nothing when we got back in the car. I tried to think of the right words but the silence did a better job of summing it up. When we reached the village I got her to stop at the all night gas station and she drove off while I was inside buying cigarettes. The attendant serving me behind the counter said hey mate, your ride's leaving. I was counting out change. I didn't even look up. I told him I had been hitching and she'd agreed to give me a lift only this far. He believed me because she was young and pretty and driving a late model sedan and because I wasn't, but there was a grain of truth in it.

I lit a cigarette as I crossed the forecourt and smoked it as I walked along trying the doors of the few cars parked on the side of the narrow road. Eventually I found a Holden with a parking ticket under the windscreen wiper and cobwebs on the side mirror and a busted lock on the passenger side. The cabin smelled damp, like rotting leather. I took the brakes off and let it coast a good mile down the hill before giving it a roll start. The engine kicked over but the heater turned out to be broken so I had to drive into town in the cold with the windows rolled down to demist the windscreen. The clutch was tricky and the engine kept wanting to stall but you expect that in an older vehicle. I was just getting the hang of it when the time came to get out.

20.

The Fantail Room wasn't really called that. Patrons gave it the name after the bird painting that hung beside the elevator. The fantails were water colours, perched on what might have been a wattle branch. While you stood waiting for the elevator you had time to work out they were both the same bird from different angles.

The building had been an insurance office originally. It dated back to the days of rigged ships and horse drawn carts. The arched windows were separated by classical columns. The Fantail Room itself was on the third floor. The protruding facade made it impossible to see inside but by standing across the road I could count the people who entered and left.

It was late evening and there was a lot of traffic. The corner intersection was busy. A bright red turbo with tinted windows and a windscreen that said "EASY BOY" pulled into the taxi stand outside the Fantail Room. Its side skirts were low enough to scrape the road, the chassis neons rippling in jellyfish colours. The driver left the engine running while he got out and put on the taxi signs. He clipped an illuminated "on duty" sign to the roof and stuck magnetic labels on the doors. He was skinny and cheaply dressed: everything had gone into the car. When the transformation was complete he climbed back inside and turned up the music. The bass was so loud it shook my stomach.

I lit another cigarette and leaned back. The locked door behind me used to lead to an underground nightclub called Warszawa that had closed a long time ago. Warszawa had mirrored walls and red velvet couches and a dance floor the size of a wardrobe. The owners went bankrupt after a drugs bust in the 80s but the club was still down there. Every now and then there were rumours that it was going to open up again. It hadn't happened yet.

Varina Sumich walked out of the Fantail Room around midnight. She was waiting for someone.

A black jeep with a camouflage top pulled into the taxi rank and Varina got inside. The jeep pulled out and caught the amber light at the intersection.

I dropped my cigarette and crossed the road. Easy Boy's duty light was on but there was no way to open the door: the rear handles had been shaved.

The driver's window slid down.

"Are you on?" I said.

"I'm working."

"I need a cab. Can you drive me?"

"This is cab," Easy Boy said.

"I want a cab."

He popped the lock.

"You get in," he said.

The back seats were buckets set in the interior roll cage. I rapped the perspex wall that separated me from the driver.

"Just drive up the hill," I said.

"Yes."

"Up the hill." I pointed again.

"I drive you."

Easy Boy punched up the music and the whole instrument panel started flashing. The black jeep was headed towards Parnell. After driving around for a good while we found the jeep parked in a side street. I gave Easy Boy a big tip. He looked at me as if I was crazy.

* * *

Parnell was just warming up. People were wandering the sidewalks in packs: guys in pressed shirts and gold neck chains; women bursting out of their little dresses. I checked out the bars and restaurants. Patrons were drinking more than they could handle and ordering food they wouldn't touch. There was a cigar bar called Fidel's the top of the street. It had a big crowd and brick walls the colour of spit but Varina didn't smoke. The singles bar next door was Club Lola, the name was squiggled across the front in neon. Inside was packed with bodies. UV lights darkened people's faces and made their hair glow. All I could see were teeth and dandruff. The floor was sticky with alcohol.

There were more UVs upstairs. The boys were loud and the girls were louder. The barmen were serving shooters on fire. The sound system was pounding out a rockabilly song. People were singing and yelling and gulping the flames.

The beer garden was open to the night. The tables were divided by trellises of plastic flowers. I walked around the shadows until I found Varina sitting behind a wall of fake roses. She had taken off her coat and pushed up her cuffs as if she was getting down to serious work. She was sitting with the raincoat woman who had met her at the Atlantic. The woman had changed her suit for a black dress with narrow mesh sleeves and a high collar that wrapped around her throat. She lit a cigarette with a blue plastic disposable before opening the yellow envelope she had in front of her.

Inside the envelope was a stack of photographs and papers. The woman started sorting through them like mail. It was difficult to see what they were from where I was standing. Some pictures were pale and others were dark. Some were snapshots and others were black and white. They were masked by dimness and the discussion was hidden by the noise of the room.

The woman took a snapshot from inside a piece of paper. It showed two girls smiling in the dappled shade. Varina Sumich and Caroline May standing arm in arm in the driveway: Varina smiling back at herself, Caroline smiling over Varina's shoulder at me. The woman unfolded the paper from around the photograph. *Missing Girl*, it said: *Missing Girl*.

Varina took the photograph from her carefully, as if it might break into pieces. She ran her thumb along its edge. Her dark hair fell across her face. She sat opposite her friend in the dark, her thoughts silent amidst the chatter of drunks and plastic plants.

* * *

The black jeep with a camouflage top was parked around the corner. I slashed the top and climbed inside and lay in the rear pan catching my breath. The reflection of Lola's blue neon wobbled in the plastic windows. The seat smelled of cigarettes and vinyl. It smelled civilised. It smelled like a girl.

There were a few items of clothing in the back. I found a yellow raincoat and a pair of leather work boots, the soles caked with dry clay. A car swept past and illuminated the compartment for a moment. I reached between the seats and opened the glove box and took out a folded road map, wadded parking receipts, a discount ferry ticket. There was a pair of sunglasses and a lipstick and a disposable camera and a comb. I found a receipt from a gas station on Waiheke Island and a bank statement addressed to a city post office box. The bank statement was sealed, so I hoped she wouldn't miss it. I tore open the envelope and checked the account details.

Varina's friend was Katie Marsden.

I knew Katie Marsden's name. I knew her smell: her perfume and her sweat. I knew she had copies of the poster. That was all I knew. But if I was right, she knew all about me.

I was thinking it through when I realised my attention had wandered to the car behind me. I had heard it drive down the street and turn. Now it had driven up behind the jeep and was sitting there with its engine running. I waited for the driver to kill the engine but it was still running. I peered over the seats. The lights were on full beam.

I played it cool. I climbed into the front and opened the door and got out and calmly walked away. I heard the driver get out of the car. She shouted something. I kept walking. Getting out of my jeep, walking up the road, going to a club: that was all I was doing. She yelled again. It wouldn't be long before somebody else heard her. I was looking around for somewhere to run when she shouted one more time.

"Mark Chamberlain?"

I turned around. I'd never seen Daisy standing upright before. When he was sitting inside his taxi cab he looked like he was part of it, or it was part of him. On his feet, he was an even bigger man with broad shoulders and a round belly that stretched his lava-lava. He stood in the glare of the Commodore's headlights, his head tipped to one side like someone had just hit it with a bat.

"Mark Chamberlain," he said again. He was certain of who I was, now. He stabbed at me with one fat finger. "Cab for you," he said.

21.

Daisy said he didn't know who booked it. A guy had just called on his cell phone and asked him to pick me up, and Daisy knew some people at Lola, and that was it. I sat back and let him drive. I didn't want to talk to him. The cab smelled like flowers that had been standing too long in the vase.

"So have you got a big boat, darling?" he said, finally. He sounded more out of it than ever.

"No. Do you?"

"Oh, goodness—not me. I drive a taxi. But there are some beautiful boats down there, you know?"

"For sure."

"Beautiful boats. All the millionaires come here for summer, you know?"

"Uh-huh."

So that was it: we were heading to the waterfront. I concentrated on breathing through my mouth. The upholstery was sticky to touch.

Daisy cut under the harbour bridge and turned onto the road that ran alongside the marina. The marina Yacht Club stood at the end of the causeway, its lights glowing under the night shadow of the bridge. I made him stop and let me out before the car park. I lit a cigarette and watched him make a five-point turn and drive back to the city at a crawl. When the headlights had disappeared, I started walking.

The causeway foundations were collared with barnacles and mussels along the tide line. The industrial part of the harbour was still working but the recreational moorings were quiet at night. Pleasure boats rocked in tidy rows. The breeze was sticky with salt.

The yacht club was built like an old motel. Christmas lights sagged along the zig zig balcony. A line of rubbish bins stood outside the kitchen. A Ducatti was padlocked in the forecourt. The outside tables were empty. The tinted windows were blurry with smoke.

The people inside were mostly men in their 50s. They sat around the tables as if they had been fitted to them. The racing was playing loudly on the corner TV. The carpet tiles were marked with burns and wet patches. There was a gold-lettered regatta scoreboard behind the bar and a line of tiny trophies on the spirits shelf. The only other colour in the room was in the faces.

The kitchen counter was serving chips and fritters. The barman was pulling beers on a fake woodgrain handle. He had a mullet and a capped front tooth and a limp. His red tie was elastic and his white shirt showed his bony shoulders. He carried a corkscrew in the pocket of his dinner suit waistcoat, its satin panels belted at the back.

I looked around for whoever I was supposed to meet. Senior Detective Harry Bishop saw me and stood up.

He had lost weight with age but his bones looked strong. There was a lot of grey in his moustache and the hair on the sides of his head. His round cheeks and nose were scribbled with broken red capillaries. His teeth were clean. His short-sleeved shirt was unbuttoned at the collar to reveal a pink triangle of sunburn. His tie was folded in the embroidered pocket that said *Guard-IT*. He wore belted grey uniform pants and polished safety shoes.

His handshake was firm. He kept hold of me for as long as it suited him. His palm was dry and his fingernails were cut square. The blue veins ran straight up his arm. He had a steady squint like he was appraising the sight of me and weathering it at the same time. The big gold machine on his wrist looked like a diver's Rolex but wasn't. I guess that was the difference between retiring and being forced to retire.

"Mark Chamberlain," he said. "You remember me?"

"It's been a long time."

"Twenty-two years." He nodded to where the taxi would have stopped. "I hope you didn't pay the fare."

"I did. Daisy never misses a trick."

"He knows people, though. *Faafafine*, right? Youngest male of the family raised as a female, in the Islands tradition."

"I heard he was half Dutch."

"He's half something." Harry winked. "You were one of the first kids I interviewed, back at the school."

"That's right."

"I insisted on interviewing all the local kids myself. I got a lot of flak for that later on. People said I was micro-managing. Which I was. It was my first major investigation. I had it planned down to the last inch. Every little thing that didn't go right was a disaster." He tapped his glass. "So I drank. I'd go to the bar at the station, or here. It hasn't changed."

He bought me a beer and ordered for himself what he said. The barman limped away.

"See that?" Harry said. "Motorcycle. The left's artificial. His old bike got crunched on the motorway between a slow van and the car he was racing. That's his Ducatti outside. He bought it with his ACC—says he's got nothing to lose, now. Do you ride?"

"No."

"Caroline's brother died on her bike. And now her mum and dad have slipped away. And that's that."

"You stayed in touch."

"As things turned out. Caroline's father retired to a property owned by one of my firm's clients—Rory Jones. What are the odds, eh?"

"Probably not that high."

"That's what I reckon. Rory's building was burgled recently. Someone buzzed the intruder in and he did four premises in a row. Very calm, cool. A professional stealing to order. He took cash, electronics: goods that were easy to move. Stole property from three and left the Mays' apartment untouched. What was that about?"

I shrugged.

"I mean, the intruder had time on his hands," Harry said. "Nobody had seen him. He wasn't interrupted. He had the run of the place. But he didn't steal anything from the Mays' house. In fact, he made a point of stopping in the room Mr. and Mrs. May kept for their missing daughter. They had all her things there. Her clothes, her dolls. Her school photos: everything arranged like a shrine. And the burglar stood there. He touched the bed, he ran his hands across the clothes in the wardrobe."

"You have his fingerprints?" I said.

Harry shook his head. "He wore gloves. But this was an old couple's place: there was dust on everything. On the clothes, the furniture. The photographs. The burglar touched the photograph of Caroline's school class," Harry said. "First he touched Caroline's face, and then he touched yours."

He reached out and touched me between the eyes.

"Caroline wrote the name of everyone in her class on the other side of the photograph. Mark Chamberlain. She picked you out."

I wanted to turn around and leave. I couldn't.

"I got a colleague to send me your criminal record," Harry said. "You're still in your mother's place. I hadn't pegged you for the sentimental type."

"She left it to me. I never felt like selling."

"I can see why. It's a nice little place. The woman who lives out the front—lovely woman. Nice dog. And the place is tidy, with a little bit of a garden—it must be worth a bit. It's central so you can walk to anywhere in town. And it's secure, right? Nobody would suspect anyone operating out of a little old granny flat: nipping out at night to steal things, stashing them inside. I had a nosey around. You've been busy. At first I was surprised to find the door unlocked but I could see the logic of it as soon as I walked in. Is anything in that apartment actually yours?"

"I have some things."

"You have a shitload, my friend. How much do you earn?"

"I don't know."

"And Lennox does all right out of it?"

I said nothing.

"Lennox Desmond Wilson," Harry said. "Major theft convictions, minor theft, receiving stolen goods. Minor assault charge from way back. He's retired, though—right?"

"I don't know."

"I mention Lennox because there was in incident recently that was his style. And something else that caught my eye out on the west coast."

"Probably just kids."

"It sounded like it, yeah. Two kids out for a good time. So who are you seeing?

"It's a small world."

"You like the older women, am I right? Like the woman you were following tonight. It took me a minute to work it out and then I realised: little Varina Sumich, all grown up. It's great that you're still so close. Does she know?"

I looked around the bar. Nobody looked back. They were all just a bunch of drunks. The only people interested in this conversation were Harry and me.

"What do you want?" I said.

"Just to talk. If you want."

"About what?"

He looked at me like he had been waiting for that question his whole life.

"About the one thing we share," he said. "Caroline May."

22.

Harry paid for a second round and carried the glasses outside onto the patio. I shut the ranch slider behind us, my reflection flashing past. It was a relief to close the greasy pane over the rest of the bar. I was rattled. The threat of Harry saying what he had in a room full of strangers was obvious. He had been following me around for weeks. Even the taxi driver he sent to collect me was a witness to the smash and grab. Whatever he wanted to talk about, I was going to listen, and he knew it.

The noise inside the Yacht Club was shaking the windows. Someone had put on a Neil Diamond track and the drinkers were shouting and carrying on. But from the outside the building floated in its own soft light, its forecourt barely a shade lighter than the night sky. The coloured balcony lights winked on and off. The traffic passing over the bridge whispered like a second sea.

Harry stood the drinks on one of the patio tables and invited me to sit down with him under its damp, striped umbrella. He knocked imaginary dust off the knee of his uniform trousers. He crossed his legs and said nothing for a while. When he spoke again he stayed facing the harbour and the dark.

"I reckon there are two cars for every boat that's tied up around here," Harry said. "You're not supposed to drink here unless you're a member, and you can't be a member unless you have a berth, but they don't give a shit. The first time I came I told the barman I was negotiating a lease. He knew I was lying."

Harry sniffed.

"I started coming here late in 1979, when the search for Caroline was starting to come off the rails. I was as white as a sheet: soft hands . . . I never told them what I did. I used a false name on the membership application. If anyone asked I told them I was in real estate. I didn't want to be recognised as the head of the big investigation that couldn't find the girl. But I realised in the end that it didn't matter. They're all soaks. The more you fuck up, the better it makes them feel about themselves. That's what makes it a great place to drink. And that's why I come here now. People like that are kind of like a reverse inspiration."

"I know the type."

Harry grinned. He turned his glass in his hands.

"I spent a lot of time here," he said. "A lot of time. The water gets dirty in summer. You dump anything in the harbour and the tides wash it right back in around here. People think it's magic but it's not. This is a small town: everything is connected. It's no surprise after such a big case to bump into people you know. It doesn't matter where you go or where you've been, you're always going to get dragged back to the one thing that shapes it all."

Harry wiped his round face.

"When I was first introduced to Caroline May, things were very simple," he said. "She was a young girl, an unlucky girl who walked out the door one day and never came back. So we covered every detail, gathered every piece of evidence we could. We went through her bedroom, her things. She had a string painting: nails hammered into black wood threaded with fine green string, like a net."

"Every kid had one of those," I said. "We made them in woodwork class. Everyone's looked the same."

"But this one was Caroline's," Harry said. "We took it away because it might have meant something. A photographer came in and shot her room from every angle. We put her underwear in plastic bags. We rubbed chemical swabs on her mattress and her pillow. We scratched paint off the sideboard. We had boxes filled with paper and numbers and photographs. People said I failed because I was an addict but they were only half right. It wasn't alcohol I was addicted to: it was evidence. Stuff. A piece of clothing, junk jewellery: it didn't matter what it was.

"Because what makes 'evidence'? Evidence looks the same as anything else. Until you say it's evidence, evidence is nothing more than a broken branch or a mark on a glass. But it has to be small enough to carry. You couldn't say the whole of North Head is evidence because it's too big. Presenting a whole street—that would be ridiculous. Yet a whole street might be evidence. The whole of North Head was part of what happened to Caroline. The weather and the houses and the spaces between the houses and the people in every house— somehow, in some tiny way, it all contributed to Caroline May's disappearance. The only way to understand it was to look at it all: every piece of it.

"Which was impossible, of course. You can never do that. So what we did was guess. We picked out little bits here and there. We looked where Caroline was last—even though the most important thing might have been where she was seven days before, or ten. Maybe, six minutes before she disappeared, maybe the wind blew off the sea and blew the hair across her eyes and that made her turn her head and she saw something—maybe that was it. We'd never know.

"We gridded North Head. We went over it with a fine-toothed comb. We looked for small things. We saw what had happened as a series of objects: that was a mistake. Because objects can be lost, like a house key. They can be put aside. They can be stolen. And yet still, that's how people insist on describing their entire lives: discrete objects, scattered and lost and then found again. Even if those things were significant in that way, what does finding them prove?"

"I don't know," I said. "I guess that's what you get paid to work out."

Harry held up a gap of the night air between his finger and thumb.

"When you go through missing persons files you see these little yellow stickers about this big with a single word on it—'recovered.' What that sticker means is that you've found some part of an individual. It doesn't mean that you've recovered emotionally, or that anything has been resolved. It just says you found something."

He smiled thinly.

"In my field of business, that qualifies as a major success."

"So you're saying you failed?"

"My team? No. We found everything about her that was there to be found, and in the end, it meant nothing. Because the real thing—the thing everyone wanted—you can't find that anywhere. Not in a shadow, not in a stranger. People were never looking for an explanation or evidence or facts. They wanted her. They wanted Caroline. And she wasn't there."

He wiped his mouth. He took the poster out of his back pocket and spread it on the table.

"And then I get this."

Missing Girl, it said. *Missing Girl.*

"You remember these, right?" Harry said. "They pasted these all over the neighbourhood. All around me, like a taunt. Hell of a coincidence that I should get one now."

I shrugged.

"Who'd have a sense of humour like that? To stuff it in the mailbox and run away. A coward, perhaps. Someone who likes to be in control. A vandal. A peeping Tom. A thief."

"I got my copy," I said.

"I delivered it. It's like a chain letter. We're all getting them."

The coloured light flickered in the wet wood. I waited.

"Mark William Chamberlain," Harry said. "First charged age 18: trespassing, breaking and entering, theft. District court conviction; fined. Second arrest a year later: trespass, breaking and entering, theft. Convicted of charges; sentence deferred. Third conviction two years later: trespass, breaking and entering, sale of stolen goods. Fined, probation, community service. Fourth arrest for burglary and associated charges: sentence suspended. Fifth arrest: multiple burglary charges. Nine months jail term, minimum security prison. Paroled after seven months. Parole staff and social workers report no criminal activity since that time. I emphasise the word 'report.' Do I have that about right?"

"Just about."

Harry bit his bottom lip for a moment.

"We have the registration of the car driven by the girl you were with in Titirangi."

"She's not involved."

"You had an argument? You broke up?"

"Something like that."

"I'm guessing you don't stay in relationships," Harry said. "I'd say a year would be the longest you've been with anyone. Six months tops. And you haven't lived with anyone—that's not a guess: I can tell that from being in your apartment. You've worked part-time only as a condition of your parole and dropped it the first chance you got. You don't work with others and you don't like being ordered around. It makes you feel like a kid which you're obviously not—at least not in years."

"What's your fucking point?"

"My point is, what you're doing with your life. If your mother hadn't left you the apartment, you'd have nothing. You're going round in circles."

My stomach flipped. My face felt hot, then cool. The music behind us changed.

"I know this pattern," he said. "You're thinking about nothing except the matter at hand. When you break into a place, you're not looking for goods. You already have goods. You're investigating these houses. You're looking in them. What for? Not for things to sell. You have plenty to sell. No, you're looking for something else. It's compulsive. You're like those men going back into the tunnels over and over even when they knew they'd find nothing."

"Bull."

"You remember her endlessly, don't you? You can remember her clothes, her hair. You remember how she smelled."

"I remember her," I said.

"You remember her over and over," Harry said. "You bring her back constantly and you roll in it and you feel good for as long as you remember. Do you know what that is, Mark? That's what therapists call a symptom of euphoric recall. You're locked into a cycle of bringing her back in your mind. You're recreating the guilt of your loss. You feel guilty, Mark—why is that?"

"Why are you telling me this? What does it have to do with you?"

"I fell on the same sword."

"And you want me to do the same."

"I could dob you in," Harry said. "That would let you off the hook. You'd be arrested for major theft. Multiple convictions: you'd go down for a long time. The system would treat you for your addiction. They'd probably blame the whole thing on your dead mother, your social background. You could sit inside for a couple of years feeling sorry for yourself and then get out, and then what? Maybe you'd be fine for a while. But Caroline still wouldn't be there."

The tassels around the striped umbrella fluttered in the breeze. The black current drifted to the side as if the waves were draining away. Harry breathed out, slowly, like he was staring back the way he had come.

"This is the nature of a search. You ask questions, but not about what you're doing. You follow procedure, but not a path. You're doing the grids, the numbers. You're doing it all by the book. And that's fine as long as you believe in what you're doing. If the search is in the right place, you'll find the answer. But if it's not . . ."

"The last day I saw you, you were drunk," I said. "You were staggering over the school grounds and staring at the girls."

"I more or less recall."

"I bet you know it step by step."

Harry's stare aged as he contemplated it. For a second, his face was creased with pain like something was passing over him: like all the days of long work registered right there. It was the strain of a weightlifter when he first meets the bar: all his weakness in one moment.

Harry put down his glass. He wiped his nose. He stood and took his grey uniform jacket off the back of the chair and slipped it on over his white shirt, straightening himself before he zipped it up. Harry took pride in his appearance. Harry was in control: of his job, his health, his drinking—everything. After twenty-two years he was still in charge of the investigation and he was letting me know that. He was still boss, no matter what happened next.

"I get an ache just before sunrise," Harry said. "I feel like I ought to be with my wife. So that's where I'm going."

"I think I'll stick around."

Harry sneered again, his lopsided, pushed out of shape grin.

"I thought you might," he said.

23.

The elevator wobbled as it went up to the Fantail Room. I slid open the cage and stepped out. The red corridor was empty. The wooden walls smelled of smoke. A crescent of spilled drinks marked where the swing doors opened and closed.

The bar inside was a trail of the night that had passed. The empty stools were crowded around the windows. The couches at the end of the room had been pushed together so the people who had been sitting on them could hear each other when they talked. Filter butts were tracked into the floor.

The glassie girl was carrying a bucket between the empty tables and filling it with Stella bottles. Her nose ring still hadn't taken. The side of her nostril was an angry pink. The oven burns on her hands had started to heal. She raised the bucket and carried it out the back, shoving the stools into position with her free hand.

A fat guy with curly hair was mopping down the counter. His name was Charles. Charles was working at the bar to pay off his student loan. He majored in classics, which would give him something to fall back on. The skin on his nose was still pink from skiing season.

Varina Sumich was still pale. She hated the sun. She checked the beer and made a note in a battered school exercise book that was hanging from the counter on a piece of grey string. Charles called to her from the till.

"Are we closing off?" he said, and he tipped his head to me. She glanced over her shoulder and then back at him.

"Yeah, close it off," she said.

"Sweet." He sprang the drawer.

Varina drained the sink. She took out some glasses and stacked them in the washing machine. She picked up a towel and wiped her hands, slowly. Her charm bracelet was spotted with water. She had pushed up her sleeves to keep them dry. She was wearing the same black clothes she'd had on at the gym. The T-shirt was greying and the jeans were white at the seams, softened by laundering and the working hours. The cuffs stopped a little short of her DMs. She was still tall for her clothes.

She put down the towel and walked over to where I was sitting.

It had been years since we had stood close. She clenched her jaw a little but after I kissed her, as I sat back, she smiled at me with something like relief. Her cheeks were pink from the hot sink water and her eyes were bright but her stare was dark— her father's stare, as much as I could recall it. She'd told me once how her mouth was too wide to be attractive. I don't think she believed that anymore.

"I remember that." I pointed to her Russian wedding ring. "It belonged to your grandmother."

"That's right." She flexed her hand. "It used to fit my middle finger. I should get it recoated. All the gold's come off."

"So you're a manager now."

"For about a year. I started after I got back from Sydney."

"Where were you there?"

"The Austin Arms. Toss-the-boss Fridays. Wet T-shirts in the beer garden Saturdays."

"Classy."

"It was alright. Dev, the owner—he was a very funny guy."

She shrugged off what she wasn't going to tell me. "But it didn't work out. And yourself?"

"I'm doing alright."

"Alright at what?"

"Odd jobs."

"I heard there was some trouble."

I thought about Harry Bishop running through my life like it was a laundry list and wondered why I couldn't do that.

"Some," I said. "Nothing bad. It happens to everyone for a bit."

"Tell me about it. I wasted a lot of years, running away. And then I came back. To work in a pub."

"It's alright."

"It's unhealthy."

"How far do you think you swam?" I said. "In total. End to end, in all the pools."

"You know, I thought about that. You can probably almost work it out." She shook her head. "All those trophies."

"But you still go swimming every morning."

"Oh, Mark," she said. "How do you know I do that?"

* * *

Charles was fussing over the till, sighing as he scooped the coins and notes from the drawer slots. He counted each stack of ten notes twice, pressing the Queen's face flat with his knuckles and flicking the corner with his thumb. When he had counted each stack he folded it in half and slipped it under a wad held by a rubber band. The notes were crumpled and the coins were dark. Money starts off smelling of ink and brass but it always ends up smelling like people.

Varina and I stared at each other. The silence stretched a long way back. There was too much for us to ever catch up on. We'd been apart a long time but nothing had changed. She was the person I remembered. She looked the same as she had leaning

on one elbow in her single bed, her homework pinned to the
moonlit wall. She didn't look angry or scared, and she didn't
look impressed. She looked like someone who had arrived much
earlier: someone I had agreed to meet but then kept waiting.

Charles wasn't enjoying the silence. He knocked the folded
bills square on the bar top, like a gavel.

"Vee?" he said. "You want me to close up?"

"Yeah," she said. "Close up." And she touched my arm like
she was putting a phone call on hold: Varina Sumich will be
with you shortly.

She went out back and got her jacket: dark green, army issue
with narrow sleeves. I told her that I preferred the one she'd
been wearing the other night and she shook her head, disap-
proving of us both.

"This better be your shout," she said.

* * *

Tokyo Joe's was one of the Japanese restaurants that stood
up by the Town Hall. It opened first as a novelty venue called
Joe's American that served burgers and Buds and played Elvis
on the jukebox. It did okay for a time. You could sit at the window and watch the boy racers on Mayoral Drive. Later when
the drivers started racing out south and business fell off and
one of the Japanese restaurant owners bought it. He painted
the place green and played tapes of Sumo wrestling on a TV in
the corner but kept the jukebox and the coffee machines. For
some reason it was the place to go if you worked in a bar.
Varina recognised someone sitting at one of the other tables. I
got a beer and sat down.

Varina ordered a coffee. The top on the sugar shaker was
crooked. She unscrewed it and scraped the hardened crystals out of the thread with the handle of her spoon as she
spoke.

"I knew someone was watching," she said. "I thought it might be you. I've often imagined that you're somewhere around. It does freak me out. But I'm getting used to it. Harry Bishop came into the bar. Did you know that?"

"I had an inkling."

"He was talking about Caroline. About you."

"What did you do?"

"Threw him out. Which I probably shouldn't have done. A guy like that is a good customer."

"You hated it when your father drank."

"He was my father."

"Were you sorry when he died?"

"I came back, didn't I?" She examined the spoon. "So you read the obituaries. Every day?"

"I read the whole thing, front to back. Everyone reads the paper when they're inside. The habit stuck."

"I never thought of that." She finished cleaning the sugar shaker and set it back against the wall.

"But you weren't surprised to see Harry."

"If anything, he was late," she said. "I've been thinking about this for so long now. Over twenty years. Which is to say, I haven't thought about it directly. I've avoided deep analysis. I avoided myself."

The line sounded rehearsed, as if she had announced it to a group. I swallowed some more beer. She rested her chin in her hand.

"Do you have a girlfriend, Mark? What does she think of all this?"

"She was interested at first. But, you know, the reality is always a little different."

"She walked out?"

"Drove, actually."

"Do you have any friends who you haven't met while you were in jail or in trouble with the law?"

I shook my head. "But I think that's pretty necessary. It saves a lot of work explaining what I do. You're maybe the one person who understands."

"I understand that you've been following me all this time," she said. "I don't understand why you're telling me about it now."

I took the piece of paper out of my pocket and unfolded it and set it on the table. *Missing Girl*, it said. *Missing Girl*.

"Harry left this for me," I said. "Someone sent one to him. I think it was your friend, Katie Marsden."

"You've seen them before. They used to be all over town. Why should it freak you out now?"

"Caroline's father died two weeks ago. Her whole family is gone."

"Like you said, you read the obituaries." Her voice was a purr. "How long did it take you to work out where they lived?"

"Not long. They set up her room in the new place. It sounded sour."

"Why shouldn't they do that?"

"They were obsessed."

"And what are we?"

"We have memories. A past. Things that happened to us both."

"And that's it?"

"Yes," I said. "The whole thing. So why is your friend sending everyone these posters?"

"Well, you tell me, Mark. You're the one watching everybody else. You're the smart guy: you tell me what you think it means."

I wanted to grab her and give her a shake. I glared at the other diners. I felt like they were listening to everything that we had said. Varina finished her coffee and set the cup down.

"There's something you should see," she said. "You'll have to come back to my place."

"You mean, while you're there?"

24.

The streets were almost empty but Varina still drove faster than she needed to. The car's old engine rattled as she chopped down a gear and ran an amber light. Our voices had become raised at Tokyo Joe's: now she just pressed down on the pedals while I stared out the window.

Her apartment was in a block on the old part of Dominion Road where the run-down shop fronts had been taken over by family businesses. The supermarket was painted red and brown and turquoise. The suit hire had been turned into a mah jong parlour. The old Starlight Theater played Bollywood movies. In the restaurant next door, a kitchen hand was unhooking glazed ducks from the window. The kids standing around smoking outside could have been about to leave or just taking a break. The neighbourhood crossed every date line, now. It never slept.

Varina parked in the 60 minute zone across the road and locked the security brace over her steering wheel.

"The traffic cops don't come round until eight, and I leave before seven to go swimming every morning," she said. "But you know that, right?"

"That brace won't stop anyone."

"No one here's going to steal it."

* * *

The entrance was around the back. The narrow alley was littered with paper wrappers and vegetable waste. Both her speed suits were drying in the stairwell. She unlocked the door at the top and stepped inside, the switch cord swinging behind her.

The flat was one and a half rooms that had been gutted and redecorated at some expense. The walls were cream and the kitchenette was Italian and the blinds were rainforest red. The bare wooden floor shined like a mirror. Beneath the varnish were little black half-moons that marked where furniture had stood forty years before. Varina's clothes hung on a standing rail behind a curtain. The bed was a futon. A stack of boring women's magazines lay next to the side that would get the sun. The single bulb in the ceiling was the still, pale kind that burns only in a place where someone lives alone.

"You want the Cook's tour? Kitchen. Lounge. Bedroom. Now I want a drink." She dumped her bag and keys on the bench and opened the fridge. "Would you like another beer?"

"I would." I peered through the blinds. The kids outside the restaurant were talking on their cell phones. "How's the duck?"

"Not bad. I eat there all the time."

"Is it noisy?"

"And getting worse every year. But it's close to town. You've got to have that."

"And no flatmates."

"I see enough people at work. And the gym." She sat down on the bed and switched on the bedside lamp and the room, gently, became larger.

"What happened your trophies?"

"I threw them out."

"All of them?"

She nodded. "When I stopped competing. When I was eighteen. I was always getting sick, from the different pools. Then I got an infection in my shoulder, and it settled on my chest. They gave me antibiotics but it came back. I actually lost my hearing, temporarily. I could only sleep on one side. When the fever broke I was in bed staring at the walls. The sheets were soaked. By the time I got better, I'd quit. My dad was furious." She closed her eyes for a moment, the argument still loud in her head.

"But you started again."

"After he died."

She uncrossed her legs and crossed them again, her bare white feet sticking out of her black jeans.

I looked at the double locks on the door, the chain. The window had been fitted with a locking bolt. She was following my gaze.

"So how would you do it?" she said.

"I wouldn't."

"Oh, come on. Be a sport."

"Through the window, maybe."

"People would see."

"What would you do if those kids down there started fighting each other? Would you call someone straight away?"

"I'd probably wait awhile."

"There you go."

"But I'm here at night. You'd be breaking in here during the day."

I shrugged. "I'd just come in through the back door."

"There are two locks."

"I could work in the stairwell, in private. It doesn't take long."

"And where would you look then?" she said. "I guess it's easy, being so small."

"Doesn't matter how big the place is," I said. "Women believe where they sleep is safe, so that's where they keep things."

"You were going to look anyway."

"In the morning. When you got up and had a shower. I'd just let my arm fall out and reach underneath."

"Casually."

I cleared my throat.

"I'm just being honest," I said.

Varina rolled the cold, sour beer in her mouth. She reached under the bed and handed me a red plastic photograph album.

A dusty poster was glued to the cover. *Missing Girl*, it said. *Missing Girl.*

"1979," she said. "The book of Caroline. I kept it while it was happening. I don't really look at it now."

I opened it. The album was filled with press clippings. The headlines were yellow and small. The first accounts were only a paragraph long because in the beginning there was so little to report. A girl had disappeared without trace. She had walked out one night and never come back, and that was it.

"I used to have dreams," Varina said. "Always the same one. She was lying on her back in the snow. Her eyes were closed, like she was sleeping. Like she was the one who was dreaming."

The plastic sheets that covered the pages had stuck to each other. They had to be peeled apart as I turned them. The photos seemed to have been taken longer ago than I remembered. The big search on North Head: the grid, the tunnels. Harry Bishop squinting down his crooked nose, his wide tie flapping in the wind. The appeals to the public: the rumours, denials. Angry letters to the editor. Harry Bishop stepping down. And then, slowly, the drip feed of anniversary stories. A year, two years. The poster photograph of Caroline appeared maybe thirty times, each time wiser and more macabre.

At first her smile was innocent, then beautiful, then sarcastic and painful in its denial and then finally nothing more than a photograph of a smiling girl: a photograph taken a long time ago.

Varina and Caroline standing in the driveway before the pine needles: Caroline smiling, Varina cut out of the frame. What she remembered. What had been lost.

"I remember this," I said. "This was on your bedroom wall."

"That was the summer before," Varina said. "Caroline's father had a camera with a self timer. We stood it on a tripod in the driveway in front of the trees. You started the timer by pressing the shutter button once. The timer was clockwork:

you could hear it whirring for ten seconds as it wound down before tripping the shutter. That's why we're laughing—we started to giggle in the time it took for the camera to fire. Caroline was the one who started the timer, so really she took the photograph. It was a self portrait."

On the last page of the album was a photograph of a mountain. The slope was white. Three black smears marked where the plane had gone down. The search grid was laid out across the snow and debris: perfect rows of flags and lines.

"Why do you have this in here?" I said.

"Because that's where she was found," Varina said.

"No, she wasn't. That was just a story."

"Some victims were never identified."

"Because they weren't carrying passports. The police knew who they were."

"But it's still possible that she was there."

"But she wasn't."

"But it was what we believed," she said. "You remember the stories. That she survived the crash: that she tried to crawl away. They said they covered it up. So relatives wouldn't be upset."

"But it's not true," I said. "None of that happened."

Varina sighed. "Do you have dreams, Mark?"

"Maybe."

She waited.

"I'm standing on a beach," I said. "I'm barefoot, and my feet are wet. And there are a hundred Carolines. There is a spray off the waves—a white spray. The Carolines are looking out to sea."

"Do they feel real? Do you feel sad, afterwards? Do you cry?"

"I don't know why you're angry at me."

"Maybe if we said she was on the plane, then she was on the plane."

"There's no evidence that she was."

"There's no evidence that she wasn't." Varina was serious now. There was no sarcasm in her voice. "Why can't it just be true, Mark? Why couldn't we just be right—even for one second? Tell me why that would be so wrong."

I didn't answer. I waited for it to pass. Varina slugged back her beer before she spoke. Her stare held me tight.

"I still care about you, Mark. I know you still care about me. After all this time we're exactly where Caroline left us. And that's the problem: we're all still in love."

25.

Josie called from the Viaduct, screaming. She was spending the night in a hotel. The suite was huge and there were mirrors in the bathroom. She could see a yacht coming in and a trawler moored to the wharf and all these birds circling the hotel, like seagulls: in fact, they probably were. The music in the background sounded like a machine.

"The sunset is amazing—can you see it?" she shouted, giggling at herself.

"I can."

"What are you doing now? You should come down. It's nice down here. You should see the bathroom."

Suddenly she roared, full-throated, the laugh ascending into a high, soft giggle.

"What's so funny?"

"I feel good. I miss you. I'd like to see you."

I thought about her sitting in the blue light.

The police kept the hot line running for a full year after Caroline disappeared. I would pick up the phone and dial the numbers once a week. I would call from other people's houses and listen, staring at the different views. After thirteen months the number changed, and the only sound that came from the receiver was the pip-pip-pip of a disconnected line. The duration of the electronic beeps was equal to the intervals between. The loop of noise was hypnotic. It was like staring at a pattern in the bright sun and seeing it in reverse after your eyes have closed.

"Are you there?" Josie said. "You're so quiet."

"I'm here."

"You haven't said anything."

"I was listening to what you were saying."

"What was I saying?"

"You were talking about the view," I said.

"That was ages ago. You're not listening to me at all. I'm just talking, blah, blah, and you're off in the clouds somewhere."

"I was remembering something you said."

"Was I being boring or something? Why are you so distant?"

"Who are you with?"

"Do you care?"

"I'm interested."

"I'm with friends. Friends who talk."

"About what?"

"Themselves. What they like. They're like the opposite of you."

The line went silent again, waiting.

Josie saying she'd been missing me was the same as her fake laugh. She was letting me know how sharp she was: the young girl, the rich girl burning a little brighter than everyone else. Now she was showing me a little more.

Josie traded in secrets. It wasn't a ploy: it was an instinct. Listening to her talk was like watching a sidewalk shell game, the truth shifting invisibly between her hands. Here's a fact—see? Now I'm going to cover it up. Now I'm going to move it around. It was what attracted me, I admit. Late at night in the gas station as she drove off in a stranger's car: Josie Richmond, disappearing.

Someone had stepped into the bathroom with her. I could hear the snap and whirr of someone taking photographs. I could hear them talking: laughing.

"I'd better let you get back to your friends," I said.

"Now you're being patronising."

"I'm not trying to be."

"When am I going to see you again? Why don't you ever invite me round?"

"My place is a mess."

Josie was silent now, feigning a sulk. I had searched her cubicle and found nothing that belonged to her. The guard at the front desk didn't care what her name was. Josie was the same as whoever she worked with. When she was with me, she broke into a house. It was how people were meant to be, now: anonymous, interchangeable.

"You're so mean to me," she said, using her baby girl voice.

"You're not wrong," I said, and hung up.

* * *

I sat drinking at the Yacht Club until the early morning. Taxis would pull up and deposit passengers, mostly men, who paused, confused, before staggering in to join the crowd at the bar. The blue night lifted and a pink light appeared behind the horizon. The last grey clouds moved apart and thinned to yellow until the cool white morning broke across the islands out in the gulf. Past the marina the neon caps on the skyscrapers weakened as the sun came up. The big billboards hanging over the motorway blanked as the reflection of the new sun took over and wiped them clean. And then the suburbs stirred and the traffic started to increase. People were driving to work, crossing on the ferries to the city. A small helicopter flew in and parked by the refinery. The wharves worked straight through, the trolley cranes whirring around the jetties like they were stirring the containers loaded up on the asphalt.

I started drinking bourbon. The barman brought out the bottle on a metal tray printed with signal flags. His stiff prosthetic walk shook the tray but he didn't spill any. He stood a clean glass beside the empties and topped it up with water that was warmer than the air. I looked back at the guys sitting around inside. Their faces were bleary with a welcoming expression, like we were all friends after sticking out the hours of piss and cigarettes and old stories. When I sipped my drink the bourbon taste was mingled with hot water and cleaning liquid.

The sun had taken a short time to rise a long way. For a moment, the fresh light made the cluttered boats seem orderly and the cement wharf clean. New cars came along the causeway looking for a park, the drivers setting out to fish or sail. A clean station wagon stopped across from the club and a couple wearing white got out. The man opened the back of the wagon and his son, who was maybe ten, climbed down. The daughter was in her teens. Her sunglasses matched her mother's. Father and son carried the chilly bin between them, the boy sloping as they walked over to the wire fence. A guy down on a fortyfooter waved and walked up the ramp to unlock the electronic gate. They chatted like old friends as he took them down to the boat and prepared to head out across the harbour's soft grey glass.

Harry Bishop was obsessed, but he was right about one thing. I had spent my whole life in the same place, going around and around. Little wonder that I was so easy to find. Harry Bishop knew everything about me now. He could wrap me up for good. It was eerie feeling like I was this close to being exposed, but I didn't feel threatened. I felt like a weight was off.

Listening to Harry made me realise what had been really going on. It wasn't about me and it wasn't even about him. All this time I thought I'd been breaking into places and stealing stuff, in fact I'd been doing the opposite. I had stepped into other people's lives and walked through their homes, but I hadn't been looking for their secrets: I had been checking on mine. I had been looking for Caroline since she left us all.

26.

I met Varina at the ferry terminal. The morning dew smelled of asphalt and salt. She bought two tickets for the Waiheke catamaran and put her arm through mine as we walked up the gangway.

The catamaran's main cabin was laid out like a factory lunch room. Plastic tables and chairs were bolted in rows on the tiled carpet and the portholes were square. There was a TV in the corner and a counter that sold wrapped sandwiches and soft drinks and black filter coffee. The other travellers all piled inside the cabin. They chewed pastries and leafed through the morning paper, ignoring the gulf as it slid past.

We sat outside. The control cabin was built across the bows so there were no seats up front. We had to sit facing backwards in the stern. The other people out back were either tourists or first-timers: a young mother with kids; an old couple taking photos.

The deck shuddered as the engines kicked into life. I watched the marina shrink as the cat pulled out from the wharf. The Yacht Club looked abandoned in the morning light but I knew it wasn't. The engine ran steady as the harbour slipped by. North Head passed us on the right, a black peak beneath the cloud.

The vessel put on speed as it entered the gulf and the water turned choppy. Spray whipped around the deck siding. Varina stayed in her seat, wrapping herself in a yellow raincoat. Auckland fell away as the outer islands rose up from the green water. North Head was the last point of land to disappear.

* * *

The ferry docked twenty minutes later. The air felt closer when we stepped onto the boards. The sounds were slower and the grass on the hills was dry. The tide line around the wharf was green with algae. There were cattle bones at the edge of the water and orange floats that had broken away from a net.

We caught a taxi to a bay on the far side of the island. Varina got the driver to stop at the bottom of a hill where the road turned into a loose metal track. The houses were hidden by the trees and scrub and the chirping of the cicadas. We walked along counting the letter boxes until we came to a cement tube that was sticking out of the wiry grey manuka. The lettering on the side said *Marsden / Williams*.

Varina pointed: "This is it."

Dandelions and puddles were growing in the bare clay driveway. The black jeep was parked at the end. Its camouflage top had been repaired where I slashed it. The house was a seventies A-frame with a porch that ran all the way around. The shingled awning was hung with different wind chimes: bamboo, glass tubes, twisted forks. Next to the house stood a shed with blacked-out windows and two stone water tanks. Beyond the tanks was a row of treetops and above them, in a straight line, a blue-green strip of sea.

The back door was open. Varina took off her raincoat and called hello as she walked inside. The chimes were ringing.

The place smelled of a log fire. The walls were covered with photographs and paintings. The glare from the sea reflected in the mountings like dozens of tiny windows.

"Katie?" Varina said. "I brought a friend."

Katie Marsden rolled over to greet us. She was stretched out in the lounge on a pile of embroidered cushions, smoking a cocktail cigarette and warming her feet in the sun. She wore a long-sleeved black top and a sarong. Daylight picked out the grey in her hair and the little lines around her mouth and the sharpness in her eyes.

"This is Mark Chamberlain," Varina told her.

"I'm so pleased." Katie's accent was Australian at the edges. Her sandals slapped as she crossed the floor. She kissed Varina and shook my hand. "Mark Chamberlain: welcome to our house. We're very pleased to have you as our guest. It's good to finally meet you in person."

"Where's Greg?" Varina said.

"In the dark room. He'll join us shortly." Katie directed her smile at me. "He still has a lot of work to do before the opening."

"These are his photos?" I said.

"Yes. From previous exhibitions. Greg doesn't sell many because he prices them so high. I think he does it deliberately. He's just signed with a new gallery and they really don't understand why he works so slowly. He insists on printing them all himself. Other professionals have assistants but Greg simply refuses. The frames are made by a gentleman who lives on the other side of the island. I've managed to pry that much away from him, at least." She smiled. "But please—you must excuse me. I'm being terribly rude. Would you care for some fresh coffee? The ferry people do their best but the stuff they serve isn't up to much."

One of the pictures showed a blonde girl sunbathing on the top of a city building. Her pool chair was in the corner of the black tar roof. Although the image was sharp there was a distinct haze in the air.

"Is this you?" I said.

"Yes. In Tokyo. Greg took that the day we met." She pointed to some of the others. "These are the markets in Singapore. And this is Shanghai. We spent a lot of time in the East."

"Some of these look out of focus."

"Yes—they're found images. Images that were made when the camera was dropped or set off accidentally. They were the beginning of his art, although we didn't realise it at the time."

I was looking at the photograph of the two girls standing in the driveway. Varina had raised her chin, nervous. She couldn't look me in the eye.

"Where did you get this?" I said.

"There are many copies of it. It's in the public domain. One was in the original police files. This print belonged to the girl's family. It was released into the public domain at the time of her father's death. Do you have one?"

"No," I said. "But I've seen it before."

"And you feel like it's yours, right?" Greg Williams said. "You feel like it belongs to you, and we stole it."

* * *

Greg had entered through the back door and was standing in the hall, smiling at us through his yellow spectacle lenses. He had a straggly salt-and-pepper beard and long hair tied back in a ponytail. He was wearing flared jeans and a bush shirt with the sleeves rolled up. There was a thin rope of coral beads around his neck and a yin and yang symbol on a leather thong. His Jesus sandals were splitting at the sole.

"He was looking at the photo you took of me in Japan," Katie said.

"She was very distracting, that day," Greg said. "I was young. Tense. I used a long lens to bring her close because I was nervous. She was a conversation hostess but she wasn't talking to me. No way. You know the first thing she said? 'You're standing in my light.' How cold is that?"

I was glaring at him. I didn't know what to say.

"Hey, listen." He put his hand on my shoulder. "Thanks for coming. Come and take a look at what we're doing."

"I don't care what you're doing."

"But you're here, right? Vee's brought you all this way, after all these years. Why don't you just come with me and check it out. Huh? How about it."

He put his hand on my shoulder. His hand felt heavy.

"It's natural to be scared."

"I'm not scared."

He smiled.

* * *

Greg's darkroom was in the shed with the blacked-out windows. The door sucked in air when he opened it. Big prints were pegged to strings across the ceiling to dry. He fished one out and held it up for me to see. Although it was a colour photograph there didn't seem to be much colour in it: a streak of blue fading into cracked white and grey. He showed me another image that was the colour of soup with a white stain in the middle.

"What are these?" I said.

He draped the print back into the tray.

"The plane crashed on Wednesday, November 28," Greg said. "The police had me on a flight down there within 24 hours. It flew to the base and we were airlifted from there to the mountain. To the event."

He shook out the fresh print and pegged it up. It was all but blank. He studied its shades of white.

"The first thing I saw was that the snow on the mountainside was totally black," he said. "Black snow. Pegged out with red and green flags flapping in the wind. The advance teams had already laid out the grid. The red flags marked a body, or part of a body. When the wind came up the red flags flapped like something dead or dying. There were birds—black gulls—circling in the sky. It was cold. My breath would freeze on the viewfinder. The focus rings on the lens kept seizing. I had to use two cameras—one warming inside my jacket and one in my hands. I kept the rolls of film under my arm so they'd turn when they were loaded. I was shaking uncontrollably. I had to use a tripod to take the photos. I had to focus by measuring, and look away as I made the exposure. I spent three days down there. All around me the people gathering material, tagging it—they had stopped looking."

"I can't imagine it."

"Nobody could." He shook his head. "One of the first things I noticed in the snow were these little boxes. I couldn't work out what they were. Little boxes gleaming in the sunlight: silver, brown boxes, shining with metal and machined glass. They were cameras—hundreds of cameras. Nearly every passenger had taken a camera on board with them to record the flight."

I looked at the prints hanging on the string.

"Have you ever taken a photograph from the air, Mark? You press the lens against the window and click the shutter. You're up high, you think you'll see lots of things. But when you get the film back from the chemist, there's almost nothing to see."

The frozen curve of the horizon. A brown pool running into blue.

"These are the passengers' photos," I said.

"Look at them. You can feel it. The warmth of the cabin. The sound of people in the seat next to you. Can you feel it? This is what they saw. Where they were."

Greg traced his finger along image. Sea and cloud and pale flat snow. The polar light from the sun was stark and bland, the warm air a blur of movement.

"Katie and I have put years into this," Greg said. "We finally managed to track them all down. You must come to the exhibition. To say goodbye—to Caroline."

"But she wasn't on the plane. That was just a story from school. Like the story that she was seen at dawn, or that she hitchhiked, or that she was murdered. They were all just stories."

"A story has to begin somewhere."

"What are you saying? You're saying it was true? You have a photograph?"

"I have something."

"What?"

"Something I can't explain." He smiled again behind his yellow spectacles. "Something you need to see with your own eyes."

27.

The exhibition was in the old post office on K Road. The only sign that the building had been converted into an art gallery was a laser-printed sign on the red front door that read *DEPARTURE LOUNGE: Photographs by Greg Williams*. A group of kids in black were smoking outside in the slanting light, the city reflected in their wraparound shades.

Varina and I waited outside.

Greg turned up in a black shirt with an *om* symbol, a fringed leather jacket with a Japanese devil across the shoulders, black pants and cowboy boots. He was carrying a camera in his satchel. Out of habit, he said, but he'd trimmed his beard and his boots were freshly shined, and I got the sense that he knew it was an important night. Katie was wearing a long dress and a scarf and laced boots that made her a little taller. She had combed her fringe so it almost covered her eyes.

The kids fell silent as we walked past. They would probably make jokes about Greg's hippy clothes after he had gone but up close his stoned smile unnerved them like a joke they didn't get.

"Are you cool?" Greg asked. I said we were.

We followed them upstairs. Varina kept pace with my silence. She squeezed my hand for a second and let go again. She had painted her nails bright red.

* * *

The carpet was chocolate. The last light of the day falling through the brown glass windows and turned the walls gold. The spiral staircase wound around a trio of oval lamp shades. There was music playing: soft electronic noises that bubbled like water.

Upstairs ran the narrow length of the building. The space had been stripped of fittings and painted white. The framed photographs hung in two lines, one down each side of the room. A movie projector stood in the center of the room on a pedestal. The rear wall was blank.

There were more than fifty guests but they had plenty of room to move. Some of them were shabby and some were old and some were dressed in expensive clothes. They looked distracted, glancing around and holding themselves in case they were being looked at. It was a typical gallery crowd, I guess: trying to look different.

Waiters were serving drinks. I scanned people's faces but didn't recognise anyone. They were just here to look.

There was a shimmer in the conversation. A thin woman broke away and walked towards us, smiling. She was wearing a black dress, black tights and red plastic clogs. Her ginger hair was cut short so it stuck up around her forehead. She had freckles and a green pinkie ring that turned out, when she shook my hand, to be a tattoo.

"Good evening, everybody" she said. "My name is Paula Shell. Welcome to The Departure Lounge."

"Hey, Paula," Greg said, and introduced us all. Paula smiled at us as quickly as she could and turned back to him. "It's so great to have you here, Greg. It's such fabulous work, so incredible. The place is just buzzing."

Katie was taking her cigarettes out of her purse.

"Oh, do you mind?" Paula said. "The gallery has a smoke-free policy."

"That's fine," Katie said in a tone that signalled that it wasn't but Paula had already turned away from her, pointing out a short man on the other side of the room. His bright green shirt had been chosen to set off his black suit but it showed up his pink face as well.

"Greg, have you met Geoff, the writer from the *Art Group*?" Paula said. "He's a wonderful guy, and he was just saying to me, how amazing these are, really exciting. I'd really like you to come and meet him."

"That would be very cool."

Katie pecked Greg on the cheek. If Paula could sense what Katie was thinking, she didn't show it. She took Greg's arm and steered him over to the critic. The guests whispering as they passed. Greg shook the critic's hand and listened to whatever he had to say with a vague smile. After what rated as a polite period another woman in black came up to the trio and introduced herself, her glass clutched to her stomach like a bouquet.

Varina came outside while Katie and I had a smoke. Katie explained that the gallery would be here for a fortnight before it moved on. The exhibitor was a collective with no permanent address. Paula Shell leased space in vacant buildings for only as long as an exhibition required and then closed up afterwards. The next show could be anywhere.

"She calls it a guerilla concept," Katie said. "She likes people to think of her like some punk revolutionary but she's actually bankrolled by her old man. That's the art world for you—the whole bourgeois thing."

It sounded like crap to me. My face said it but I didn't. Katie blew smoke to one side. Her voice was low and steady like a trainer calming an animal.

"You're still angry," she said. "It's a natural response. You've had no real therapy after your loss: no acknowledgement of grief. You've been working so hard trying to make sense of it: collecting experiences, looking for answers. The reality is much more complex. That's what you're feeling now—both of you."

Varina was staring up at the tops of the buildings.

"But it'll be over soon, right?" I said.

Katie smiled as if she had fed me the words herself.

* * *

When we went back up Harry Bishop was blocking the top of the stairs, holding a drink and looking fidgety.

"So what do you reckon?" he asked me.

"I don't know," I said. "I'm not big on art."

He wiped his face. He was not handling things so well now that there really was nothing more than orange juice in the glass. Katie stood calmly beside me. Varina stayed back a step.

"There's wine on the table," I said.

"I stopped drinking, remember?" he snapped, staring at Varina. "I've got that under control."

"Is your wife here?"

"She had something else on." He turned to Katie. "Greg Williams worked for the department once, back in the day. I should've known."

"He remembers you," Katie said.

"And I remember him," Harry said. "A pseudo intellectual. Always a little better than everybody else."

"I have to thank you for distributing our invitation," Katie said, calmly. "Greg wasn't sure about involving the authorities, but I was confident you'd track everybody down."

"Were you, now."

"Yes, I was. If it wasn't for you, Mark wouldn't be here."

Harry broke into a smile. He was furious. "So what are we meant to be looking at, here?"

"That's always the question, isn't it?"

She slipped past and into the crowd. He looked like he wanted to snap her in half. And then Varina sighed and pushed past as well. I saw him mutter something at her and she turned and went at him, right in his face, and he flinched like he suddenly wasn't sure whether he wanted a bite of her or not. Some of the guests looked around when they heard the shouting. Neither Varina nor Harry was going to back down. Finally—quickly— they came to a standstill and stood there, glaring eye to eye.

"You should be used to drunks," he snarled.

"It's my night off," she said, and turned on her heel.

I hesitated. I almost felt bad for him. His hands were shaking and he was looking around, searching for something he could get a handle on.

"I don't know what you're doing here," he said. "I always thought were smarter than this."

"So did I."

"Look at you—all lined up for your little answers. She's not here. She was never there," he said, pointing at the photos. "Ninety per cent of the population die within ten miles of their birthplace—did you know that? You. Me. All of us. We're not going anywhere."

* * *

I found Varina standing alone on the other side of the room, looking at the photographs. I stood behind her and she leaned into me and I held her hand.

The images were all similar. The altitude and glare had reduced any details to frail suggestions, like whispers: cobwebbed cracks in the ice; the deep ocean fading to a stain; a giant wave like a white eyelid. Vast landmarks left only flecks in the milk and blue ink. The air in between was silent. Even the sunlight was muted, sharpened only by the edges of a window or a wing.

I found myself staring at them and thinking of nothing. It was hypnotic: like going back to the Mays' apartment and seeing the photograph of Caroline again for the first time. I blinked. I looked around. People were milling between the parallel lines of photographs hanging on the gallery wall.

And then I got it. On either side of the long, narrow gallery space, the photographs had been hung where the windows of the airplane would have been. The position wasn't accurate: the gallery was wider than the plane's fuselage and not nearly as long, and people were standing instead of being seated. But the intention was clear. We were all looking out: seeing what they saw; breathing the same cold air.

The lights went dim.

28.

The room fell quiet.

"Here we go," Varina said.

The only illumination was a light on the bare white wall. The audience gathered around it. Paula Shell led Greg in to the middle of the circle. When she began to speak, he stopped her. She backed away and left him standing alone.

Varina stood closer to me.

Greg cleared his throat.

"A photograph is a record of what the photographer is looking at," he began. "That's the positive. Everything they're not seeing, what they don't know—that's the negative. Not the film negative: the negative in time and space that surrounds the image. This exhibition is about the negative. This is about what you don't see here—and who."

I looked around. Harry was standing at the side of the room, alone.

"The film I'm about to show you is very old," Greg said. "I made it myself. When I went down there, to the ice, I took a movie camera. I was shocked, naturally. And my hands were cold, and I was unfamiliar with the camera's mechanism. I thought the film was ruined. After I got back, I found that wasn't the case."

Someone coughed. Greg paused for a second.

"In the years since then, I've heard a lot of stories about what we were supposed to have found," he said. "Stories people told each other. Reports, even; articles that ran on the news. Hardly any of them are supported by evidence. But they all represent the truth, in a way."

It was impossible for Greg to be able to see across the room with the light in his eyes but just for a moment I thought he was staring right at Varina and me.

"We know what happened but we don't really know, and so we fill that space with what we want or what we fear, or what other people tell us. We transpose other losses onto an event to give it meaning: something to explain the grief; to conclude it. But we can't. We can't embrace it because it's finished. It's over. And it never ends. We look to the negative to explain things: to show us what we can't see."

Paula clapped. Nobody took it up.

Greg fitted the film onto the projector. The reel was the size of his palm. He fed the white leader into the guides behind the lens. The room remained silent. His movements were automatic. He threaded film and loaded cameras in a dark room: he could cue up a projector with his eyes shut.

Varina took my hand. She looked as if she was going to fall down. I pulled her close. We had all been working up to this moment without knowing what it would actually be. No one had seen the film before. No one knew.

Greg switched on the projector.

Varina held tight.

The projector bulb was the only light in the room. Scratches flickered across the wall, sparkling like neon, and then disappeared. A grey square appeared on the brick and then changed to black. The black shape shimmered. What seemed like detail was the pattern of the brickwork showing through the black light.

Nobody moved.

The projector rattled. I could smell the hot air and the celluloid moving through the gate. We all watched the black square, breathless. Varina's grip tightened as the blackness ran on. Slowly we started to understand. The film had never been exposed. There was nothing on it. But nobody spoke or laughed or moved. We were all watching, waiting, thousands of feet above the ice and snow, the dry air in our ears, the music over the headphones. The gallery was still. The only movement was the turning reels and the clatter of the machine. And then the film ended and ran off the spool and the light was released to pour through the lens and the room was filled with white.

Everyone waited. The projector engine rattled and the smell of smoke rose up. The strip of film was whipping around the spool, fluttering in the magnified light of the naked bulb. The reel had ended but nobody was moving because we could all see it now: the thing the film couldn't show. It was all around us, on the walls and the ceiling, spilling out from the back wall. Varina was standing with her hand on her mouth. The tears were running down the shadows below her eyes but she didn't wipe them away. Harry was leaning forward, his big hands clutching his little glass of orange juice, his back bowed with the weight of years.

My hands were shaking. My whole body was shaking.

Greg Williams was smiling, sadly, his own tears coloured by his yellow spectacles.

Varina was wobbling like a blade in the wind, her hot face buried in my neck, her hand holding my stomach. Because suddenly just for a moment we were right: she was there, stretched out in the ice and snow.

"There she is," I said.

The room and everyone in it was soaked in brilliant, incandescent blonde.

29.

Blonde. Caroline May had long blonde hair.

I poked my outstretched hand through it and drew downwards, straining so the smell came away in my fingers. Caroline was not the tallest girl but she was tall enough to lose yourself in.

We were close. We lived on the same narrow stretch of land around the head. We slid closer by increments until my tongue was in her mouth and she could reach around and stroke my neck and back bringing us closer still, as close as the music.

The light on the alarm unit was flashing above the lounge window like a landing signal. Clicking, red, but nobody came.

The alarm's broken, she said. Dad says he's going to fix it but he never does.

And I could see the light in her eyes: the red, and the green.

"Do you surf?" she said.

It was one of the last things she would say to me or anyone else.

I said no. She opened her mouth.

She tasted different from what I expected.

* * *

Someone pointed her out on the first day of the year. Caroline May, they said, and I looked around as she entered the room. She dumped her satchel on the chair and took out her pencil bag tattooed with blue ballpoint and typing white-out. She had lost her freckles.

The room was noisy with talk and kids rocking in their chairs. Caroline was talking to the other girls. She was wearing her sweater on a warm day, the sleeves pushed up and her shirt cuffs folded back. She had pierced her ears over summer. She wore little studs in the lobes, the sort the chemist gave out free with the piercing.

I watched her taking notes and wondered what her hand-writing was like. I guessed large and cursive, fairly tidy. She was using green ink, like half the girls in the class.

We were the same age but I was seeing her differently now, and I couldn't figure why I hadn't before. Noticing Caroline made me wonder if I'd missed something else.

It took months before we got close enough. It happened at a beach party around North Head. It started at sunset around one of the illegal bonfires the residents never reported and moved up the hill when the tide came in and threatened the flames. We ended up in the tunnels with the older kids, following the light of the torches and candles.

We smoked dope and cigarettes and passed around beer cans and a bottle of Jack Daniels. The older kids had a tape deck that ran on six batteries for three and a half cassettes. They played The Cars and the Scavengers and Cheap Trick. When the tapes started hissing they turned on the radio and Caroline went outside. I followed her. We talked on the cold side of the head and sat close and bumped hips and held hands and I kissed her for the first time. It was late May and she smiled and said: I was wondering how long it would take you to do that.

We made it home before midnight, before winter proper hit and the rains rolled in and we turned seventeen. People didn't know we were going out because we weren't. We just knew each other. I couldn't think how to describe it. I used to wait for her, and then we would hold hands in the dark some place neither of us was supposed to be. We kissed when we couldn't see each other.

I couldn't remember if that first night was starry. I remembered it that way but I might have been imagining it.

She plaited her hair for the colder weather. I imagined holding and undoing it, unthreading it around my finger in a reverse twist like a fraying rope.

The nights became warmer. Windless midnights settled in the valley. When it got too hot to sleep I sat up looking out the bedroom window counting rooftops in the moonlight. I pushed the window open. The air smelled like spring.

The feeling I got looking at Caroline was the feeling I got standing outside a house at night and looking inside: a feeling of belonging that I couldn't touch, and would never really know.

* * *

We rolled over in the lounge. We kissed. We pashed. We necked. We swapped spit. The music was playing loud. Each time the record came to the end of the side the arm clicked up and floated back to the beginning and lowered itself, wobbling, until the vinyl crackled and the songs started over. I licked her ears, the waxy trail of her hearing. I bit her lips, gently, and then hard and she giggled and said no and pulled me closer. I stroked her breast and felt her warm skin. The nipple hardened, then went soft. I made a clumsy reach around her bra, her back. She wouldn't let me remove it. She let me touch it. She liked it. She didn't care.

She put her thumb and forefinger in her mouth and pulled the rubber bands off her braces and dropped them on the coffee table: one red, one green. When we kissed again I could taste where the wires had cut: the metallic taste of blood. She smiled and cupped the back of my neck and I pressed down on her again. She opened wider and she tasted different. The room smelled of our sweat and our clothes and the old carpet and the cold salt air. The sunlight falling through the thin clouds was bright but weakened as if it had travelled a long way to get there.

I traced the smoothness under Caroline's blouse. Her shoulders were round. The inoculation on her shoulder was a tiny crater on a soft moon. She shifted her arm as I unbuttoned her top and touched her stomach. We started kissing again. We both had a sense it should go somewhere and it would, but not here. We weren't going to fuck now but we weren't going to stop. Kissing was like talking or chewing gum except I was hard and she was warm.

There was a birthmark to the left of her navel: a purple patch on her belly. Her scar was on the calf of her leg, hidden by her jeans. She had been riding when the cuff of her elephant bells caught in the chain and sucked her leg into the gear teeth. My only scar was the one on my thumb: the half-print where I had put it through the glass, horsing around on my birthday after too many beers. It was good, but it wasn't as good as the one on her leg. It was pink, and it tingled in the cold weather. She said hers itched, sometimes. I ran my thumb along it.

"Can you feel that?" I said.

The whites of her eyes deepened as she watched me. I held her knee and then her thigh. I stroked her bare navel. She started to laugh, puffing hot air on my hand. I made a grab at her belly. She squealed and clapped her hands on her stomach. I grabbed her harder and she wrenched around and pushed up. She had almost lifted me off before I realised she was strong enough to do it. I fought back and she dropped me. We wrestled on the floor, laughing. When I really pushed she was no match: she folded. It was like the last yard in a sprint: I always knew I could close it.

"Let go," she said.

"No way."

"I have to pee."

"So do it."

"I mean it."

I made a bridge with my arms and she slid out from under it. She sat on her knees on the floor for a while, looking at me with a dumb smile and then stood up and walked out. I lay on the couch. I heard the latch on the bathroom door. Girls always did that. You would hold them and kiss them and afterwards they would wrap themselves in the sheets, always keeping something back for themselves, or for someone else.

Her blouse was done up when she came back into the lounge.

"Come back and sit down," I said.

"Not now."

"You want to stop?"

"We're not really doing anything."

She stood at the window. She was looking out at the neighbourhood on the other side of the glass: the old houses and trees, the street.

"So come back," I said.

"I don't really feel like it."

"I bet you do later."

She made a face.

"You will," I said. "You always do."

I started putting on my shoes.

"When do you want to get together again?" I said.

"Maybe not for a while."

"Do you have stuff to do?"

"Kind of."

"Are you going away?"

"Don't know."

"With someone or by yourself?"

"Don't know."

"For how long?"

"It doesn't matter."

"It does to me."

She reached behind her head and bunched her hair into a single plait. I could see the goose bumps on her nape.

"You can't tell," she said. "Promise you won't."

"I can keep a secret."

"I know. I really like that about you."

The stereo crackled. The playing arm moved across and lowered itself again, and the songs started over.

"It's time to go," she said.

She let me out through the kitchen door at the back, holding the screen door so it didn't slam. When I got to the bottom of the lawn I stopped and looked back. Caroline was watching me through the wire mesh. I lifted my hand but without energy: it was more of a signal than a wave. I think she smiled. It was hard to see. She touched her fingers to her mouth and blew me a kiss through the mesh before stepping back into the darkness of the afternoon.

30.

The ferry is still the quickest way to get from the city to the north shore. The old villas still stand along the beachfront watching the boats come in but the old tin shed that used to cover the jetty was torn down years ago. It started to look eerie and dark after Caroline May disappeared: a symbol of decay and neglect and the rot of the mystery itself. Now it's been replaced by a bright new shed—a development—filled with shops that sell souvenirs. There is a fusion restaurant and a juice stand. The lights are fluorescent, and the floor is tiled with blue carpet and the air conditioning is louder than the sound of the waves.

The streets had changed since I walked along them last. The fences were taller. The cars were brand new. There were satellite dishes and TV aerials growing on everything. People in the township were drinking coffees on the sidewalk.

I climbed the head one last time. As I got higher I saw more of the horizon and caught more wind coming off the blue sea. The sky was dark and the trees around the base of the hill were shaking but there was no rain, yet, and it wasn't cold. It was a summer storm. I walked out an overhang that was short of the peak to look down at the rocks and surf. The shoreline was all broken up. The wind tasted of salt and scrub and flax.

Twenty or so years on, the property surrounding North Head has become worth a lot of money. Real estate is big business there, now. Developers moved in. The hippies and retirees sold up and left. Even the old fire station where Harry Bishop set up his headquarters was reclassified as residential and converted to apartments. The windows are double-glazed now and there are gardens planted out the front. The bamboo around the back has been dug out and the inside of the building has been painted white.

Harry Bishop never realised how appropriate it was to choose the fire station as the headquarters for the search for Caroline. For all the defenses installed on North Head, for all its fear of invasion, the only settlers who died violently in its shadow were consumed by flames. The wooden boats and wooden villas burned like tinder: it was the fire station, traditionally, that had always been the first real line of defence.

* * *

It was Friday midnight on K Road but it was still a school night. Kids were queuing up for clubs that were darker than the hour. The bouncers pretended to check IDs before letting them in. You could get twenty dollars for a driver's licence now: thirty, if there was something big on that weekend. I stopped at the gas station and stared into the security camera before buying myself a king size slab of chocolate and some cigarettes. I put them both in my bag and wandered up the street slowly, holding the bag carefully so it didn't swing.

The lights were off in the old Post Office. I walked around to the loading bay and cupped a pocket torch against the window. The only furniture in Paula Shell's office was a desk and a swivel chair and a filing cabinet. There were exhibition posters on the walls. The light was shaded by a Chinese lantern. The glazing was reinforced with a fine wire grid running through it. I found a section of clay drain pipe a little way down the road and slid it over my forearm like a glove. I smashed out the frame. The dance music from across the street hid the noise.

The broken pane was just big enough to climb through. I carefully lowered my bag onto the desk and then rolled inside. I dropped onto the floor and lay there catching my breath, staring at the ceiling.

The ground floor smelled of cement dust. The office was still in the process of being renovated to match the space upstairs. The old mail room on the other side of the door had yet to be dismantled. The floor was littered with building debris. The red steel pigeonholes had been stuffed with nails and off-cuts and plastic wrappers. There was a battery smoke alarm installed in each room. I rolled Paula's swivel chair into the room and stood on it to remove their batteries.

The gallery safe was waiting in the ambient glow of the traffic and the moon. It was five-walled with a handle and a keypad in the center of a polished door plate. I ran my hands around the cold steel back, embracing it. It was as broad as my chest, and unmoving.

I tested the handle. "You'd be surprised how often people don't shut it properly," Lennox had said. "Sometimes you just tap the thing and it's already open." It wasn't.

I took the tin of window putty out of the bag. Lennox had advised purchasing a standard product. I had chosen a special kind imported from Italy. I packed the putty around the door of the safe, sealing the crack between the door and the frame. Lennox had said to use gloves so I didn't leave fingerprints. I used my bare hands.

I left a gap at the top. I unwrapped the chocolate bar and spread the wrapping foil on the floor. I smoothed the foil flat and folded it lengthways to make a funnel that I slid into the gap at the top of the door. I packed more putty around it to keep it in place.

Then, slowly, I took the bottle of nitroglycerine out of the bag.

Lennox kept a supply of it stashed in an old spare tyre in the back of his garage. He said he got it from one of his old army mates who worked in supplies. "He can get you some good camo netting too," Lennox said as he measured some out into a jar for me, like moonshine. I didn't like the idea of carrying it as I walked around but he promised it would be okay. "Just don't go crazy with it," he said as he handed it over. "You'll only need about a quarter of that."

I tilted the jar in the darkness. The clear liquid inside looked like vodka. When I unscrewed the lid it smelled faintly of nuts.

I let a quarter trickle into the funnel, then a third, then half. I kept pouring until it was all gone. I stood the empty jar on top of the safe.

I pressed a blasting cap into the putty at the base of the frame. My hands were shaking and I was getting flustered, remembering Lennox's instructions. The task suddenly seemed like fussy work. It was tricky pouring the explosive in. It was fucking dangerous. I was sweating so badly that I could feel it running below my arms.

I lit the fuse on the cap and ran into the next room. I wasn't scared: I wanted to run. I didn't want to be there. I wanted to be somewhere else.

There was a tiny gap in time between the flash of the blast and the noise: a moment. The office door blew open and slammed shut and blew open again, sagging on its hinges as flames shot out.

Smoke tumbled through the building. I waved it away. The swivel chair was lying on its side, the castors sticking up in the air. Black streaks on the floor of the mail room fanned out from the open safe, the soot pointing to the blast. The metal door was wide open. The shelves inside the armoured casing were flickering as their contents burned. Blue flames and smoke curled up from the negatives. The reel of 8mm film was unlooping, loosening as it was consumed by its own heat. Freed, it spooled out like a broken clock spring, all tension gone. It was melting frame by frame, all monochrome implication, all unshown details erased.

I dipped my finger in the soot and wrote Harry Bishop's name on the wall and then pressed my hand beneath it, palm up, fingers outstretched: a perfect set of prints.

I left the same way I came in.

31.

There's so much to organise before you go away. You have to pack. You have to decide what you're going to need and what you can afford to leave behind. Experienced travellers say you should travel light. Others like to take everything with them but I think it's best to go pretty much as you are. Whatever you need you'll probably be able to find it further down the line, no matter where you're going.

I'm not sure what sort of traveller I'll turn out to be. I have never taken a really long trip. I've taken breaks now and then, but I've never been away long enough to consider what would happen if I never came back. I blame this on a combination of circumstances: personal commitments. But now, I guess, I'm free to go. All I need to do is to work out where I want to be.

People with experience say a journey is best approached without a destination in mind. They say it's the experience of travelling that is truly valuable: the getting there that is the fun. It's the excitement of doing something new. If you're in a different location, maybe you can be different.

The list of people you need to say goodbye to is not long. It's not the number of people on the list, but the names. And even a few goodbyes can be too much. There's so much in your head, and there's just not enough time. You rush, trying to get things done. You feel anxious because you're leaving: you experience a kind of guilt. In the end, however, you just have to let go. You have to say: this is it. I'm going.

I'm gone.

You pack your things. You say goodbye to your friends. You catch a cab to the airport. You go through the gate. You feel safe while you're waiting to board the flight. There are empty couches and potted palms and soft music, and the people on the other side look calm. You are no longer in the country, but you haven't left. You're in limbo. What happens from then on is neither real or unreal, proven or disproved. It is a period of transition and quietude; of something and nothing.

Welcome to the departure lounge.

* * *

I climbed out of the building and walked up the road. My hands were burned and my clothes smelled of smoke. I couldn't go into a bar looking like I did but it was too early to go home. The police would need time to track down Harry Bishop and find out where I lived and count everything inside my apartment and trace all the serial numbers, and that would take at least the rest of the night.

I walked around Ponsonby for a few hours. The backstreets were eerily quiet. The houses stood in an orderly line. Some of the apartment residents hadn't even bothered to lock their gate. I saw a woman taking a shower, soaping her pink arms in the open window. She was singing something. The steam curled upwards in the night, clinging to nothing as it cooled. The rest of the night was beginning to stick. A breeze was blowing in from the west.

I headed back into the city around dawn. There was parking for the staff at the Fantail Room on the ground floor of the building. I slipped the lock and waited in Varina's space. She pulled in around nine with her hair still wet from the pool. She unlocked the lift and took us up.

I bought some more cigarettes from the machine and sat by the window. Dust danced up the velvet curtains. Varina ordered in some coffee. She asked why there was ash under my fingernails. She didn't like the answer.

* * *

The trial, when it came, would not go well. I had betrayed myself as a recidivist. The court would have no choice but to hand down a sentence as a deterrent.

I broke into places without thinking of the consequences because there were no consequences, only the action of entering. Windows opened for me like doors, lock tumblers rolled to one side, cars drove themselves. That was what I did and I had never stopped to think why, not once in a lifetime of doing it. I slept during the day and walked around at night and my world was transparent. I hadn't come here to catch up. I had never left.

I started to zone out when the judge was reading the sentence. I was already in another place. I was sick of hanging around.

There were counselling later, of course. Analysis was part of the deal. There would be sessions structured in the same way as the ones we had to attend after Caroline disappeared. And so for the second time I found myself in a circle and playing along, and when my turn came I stood up straight and declared the same symptoms, and for the second time there was some truth to it. It's a standard approach. No matter what has happened, all you have to do is stand up and talk. Because all traumas are equal, now: all losses the same. It's how people are meant to be: anonymous, interchangeable.

Later came a sentencing appeal that I funded by finally getting around to selling my mother's house, which was really why, I think, she'd left to me. The developers paid an arm and a leg so they could demolish the duplex and put up another block of apartments. There were height restrictions on the site but they would ignore those. All they had to do was wait for Mrs. Callaghan—and as far as I know they're still waiting. Mrs: C is in excellent health. Which is often the case with senile dementia: it's easy on the heart.

Harry Bishop was commended by the police for providing information leading to a major burglary arrest and conviction.

Lennox was not associated with the theft because the jam shot had burned the contents of the safe. Although I had obviously been influenced by the elder criminal, the prosecution argued, my lack of expertise was evidence that I had acted alone. In his witness statement, and to laughter in court, Lennox testified that the jam shot was a lost art, now. The new bastards were built so tight, nothing's going to open them. He raised his chin a little as he walked past me on his way out. But he never got in touch.

Of course, the jam shot had turned out exactly how I wanted. By burning the film and the negatives I had finished it for everybody. The images were a borrowed moment: an aberration. The burning only completed what should have been.

As for the film: well, I'm glad that I saw it, and that Varina was there, and that I felt what I did when the glare from the reflector bulb burst through the blackness and filled the room. I still don't know if I really saw what I saw, or if it meant what I thought it did, but I had seen Varina crying and I had seen the look on Harry Bishop's face and I'm pretty sure I was right.

Paula Shell got good publicity after her gallery was broken into. The damage was covered by insurance and Daddy leased her a new place to be. Katie Marsden was not pleased to see all her work go up in smoke but Greg Williams was cool about it. He believed art, after all, was about what it didn't show: what it couldn't capture. Like fire. Like light. Like the past. For it to be gone, man: maybe that's what it is to be there. I appeared twice in court: once to plead guilty, and once for sentencing, and Greg was the only person who attended both times. We stood out in the little secure area out the back smoking cigarettes. All you are is your breath, he told me as he blew smoke. Light and air, man: we're lightweight.

* * *

Varina and Caroline photographed themselves on the day they were sent home from the beach.

"We had a game we liked to play," Varina told me. "Caroline would swim out as far as she could, and scream, and pretend to be drowning. And I would swim out and pretend to save her. I would put her in a rescue hold and swim back, holding her up. She would keeps her eyes shut and pretended to be unconscious, and I would drag her up on the sand, and pretend to bring her round. And of course, one day, someone noticed that we'd done it before: one of the parents on the beach. We stood around shivering while they yelled at us. And then we walked home. We walked back slowly, talking, with our towels wrapped around us. Her family were out. We took her father's camera and set it up and stood together against the trees. It was summer. The tar on the driveway was hot. We could hardly hear each other over the cicadas. The trees were green."

Varina folded her arms and leaned on the table. The corner of the Fantail Room was filled with smoke. My cigarettes had run out.

"What are you going to do now?" I asked her. "Will you go back to Sydney?"

"I think I'll stay," she said. "I don't like moving around."

It was late morning now and we had run out of things to say. I had a sick feeling the pit of my stomach from staying up so late for so long. We both knew what was coming next.

Varina came down with me in the elevator and unlocked the front door of the building. It had started to rain while we were inside. The cold front that was still off the west coast at dawn had blown into the city and it was beginning to sheet down. People were running across the pedestrian crossing holding their collars around their necks. The cars had their windscreen wipers going as they drove through the puddles.

"I guess summer's here," I said.

I turned round and put my arms around her and she started to cry. Her neck was hot. I held her tight.

"You always leave me in the morning," she said.

* * *

I caught a bus. The driver said good morning and I paid my fare and the doors hissed shut. It was packed. The air stank of wet coats and sweat. I found a seat down the back.

It was cold on board but it began to get warmer. The engine turned. The sun was flashing between the clouds. The rain was pelting on the glass. The passengers rested back, gently rocked by the motion. Two schoolgirls were sitting across the aisle listening to the same set of headphones. They wore blue uniforms and white socks and their hair was tied with regulation neatness. The first one was staring into the middle distance; the second was resting against the glass, staring at the movement flashing by. Their lips moved silently to the same song, mouthing the same words. They both wore a gentle expression, oblivious to the noise and the people around them, and to time. Their smiles drifted as they were carried away by the music only they could hear. They looked young because they were young. They were lost to the world.

Files have been written about what might have happened to Caroline: profiles, schedules, maps ruled with blue pencil. It's all conjecture: guesswork. You might as well consult the tarot. The only thing you can be sure of is her absence. No fact would modify that; no piece of evidence.

She rolled over. She walked out. She left. Caroline was somewhere else, now, visiting: a tourist. A traveller hearing a different language, seeing different sights.

When a plane is far away it looks like it's hardly moving at all. As it comes closer, its speed becomes apparent. Once you're on board, it seems to slow again.

I like this riddle. I turn it over in my head. I like riddles in general. I admire their circular pattern of renewal: beginning and ending, then beginning again.

It is cold, flying over the South Pole. The white flight line travels along the Ross Dependency and east across the Ballery Islands towards the Admiralty Range at the tip of Victoria Land, west of the Ross Sea. The plane drops from 16,000 to 2,000 feet and comes in low along McMurdo Sound, a forty-mile wide valley scooped out of the blue-white rock and ice: chilled and gleaming and pristine. The high sun casts no shadows. The air was still.

I leaned against the glass. I looked at the clouds. It was dark outside the window. It was bright.

ABOUT THE AUTHOR

Chad Taylor lives and works in New Zealand. He is the author of four novels—*Pack of Lies*, *Heaven* (a Miramax film), *Shirker* and *Electric*—and one collection of short stories, *The Man Who Wasn't Feeling Himself*. In 2001 he was awarded a Buddle Findlay Sargeson Fellowship for literature, and in 2003 he was the Auckland University Literary Fellow. The *New Zealand Listener* recently chose him as one of the ten best New Zealand novelists under forty.